April's menu
BARONESSA GELATERIA
in Boston's North End

In addition to our regular flavors of
Italian gelato, this month we are featuring:

- **Heart-shaped confections**

  Rita reveled in her secret admirer's delightful
  surprises—a pewter heart pin, silver charm
  bracelet and crystal heart paperweight. The
  trinkets touched her, but made her wonder:
  Just who was the mysterious gift giver?

- **Chocolate lovers' supreme**

  In dark suits that outlined his
  masculine physique, chestnut-haired
  Dr. Matthew Grayson was near perfection,
  the epitome of a refined, tasteful man.
  Why, then, did he bring out the earthy,
  naughty side of nurse Rita?

- **Steaming-hot espresso**

  One kiss… That was all Rita wanted. Just to
  feel Matthew's lips against hers and to fantasize
  about him taking her innocence. But when she
  kissed him, the brooding doctor stole more
  than just her virtue….

  Buon appetito!

Elizabeth Bevarly

TAMING THE BEASTLY MD

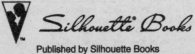

Published by Silhouette Books
America's Publisher of Contemporary Romance

Special thanks and acknowledgment are given to
Elizabeth Bevarly for her contribution to the
DYNASTIES: THE BARONES series.

For Gail Chasan.
Thanks for the memories (and so much more).

For nurses everywhere.
(Especially my favorite, Lisa Dobson.)

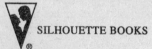

SILHOUETTE BOOKS

ISBN-13: 978-0-373-36077-2
ISBN-10:   0-373-36077-0

TAMING THE BEASTLY MD

Visit Silhouette Books at www.eHarlequin.com

Printed in U.S.A.

ELIZABETH BEVARLY

RITA® Award finalist Elizabeth Bevarly is the author of more than fifty works of contemporary romance. Her books consistently appear on the *USA TODAY* bestseller list and the Waldenbooks Romance and Mass Market bestseller lists, and her last book for Avon, *The Thing About Men,* was a *New York Times* Extended List bestseller. Her books have been translated into two dozen languages and sold in three dozen countries, and there are more than seven million copies of her books in print worldwide. She lives in her native Kentucky with her husband and son, and two very troubled cats.

DYNASTIES:
THE
BARONES

Meet the Barones of Boston—
an elite clan caught in a web of danger,
deceit...and desire!

Who's Who in
TAMING THE BEASTLY MD

Matthew Grayson—Though he was raised with wealth
and privilege, his past has left him with scars—some
visible and some private. He exudes a gruff, arrogant
confidence, but just who is the *real* Matthew
Grayson?

Rita Barone—Despite her sizable trust fund, she's
dedicated her life to nursing. But has her secret
admirer revealed the sensual woman living undercover
inside her?

Emily Barone—This young Barone cousin knows
all about keeping her feelings inside, hidden and
alone....

Prologue

There was no disputing the fact that surly Boston winters tended to slow things down in the emergency rooms of the city's hospitals. But that only meant it wasn't standing room only, Rita Barone thought as she gazed at the still-bustling E.R. this bitter early February morning. There was plenty here to keep the staff busy. Certainly enough to make her wish she hadn't picked up the shift to help out one of the other nurses. Normally, she worked in the coronary care unit, which was a walk in the park compared to the E.R. Still, Rita had started in the E.R. at Boston General, so in a way, this was like coming home.

At home, though, she didn't have to treat overblown cold sores and ingrown toenails. No, when Rita went home—home to the big Beacon Hill townhouse where she'd grown up, and not the North End brownstone she shared with two of her sisters—her parents pampered her like a princess. In fact, she could be living the life of a princess at this very moment had she chosen, since each of the Barone siblings had collected a million-dollar trust upon turning twenty-one. But Rita, crazy as it might sound, had wanted to be a nurse instead of a princess. Now, after almost three years of employment at Boston General, she knew she had made the right choice. Princesses, she knew, hardly ever saved lives. Plus, they didn't have nearly as good a health plan as she did.

Cold sores and ingrown toenails, here I come, she thought wryly now as she leveled an espresso-colored gaze on the wretched refuse cluttering the E.R. waiting room. The people seemed not to have changed one bit since she had been a regular staff member here.

But then, she hadn't changed much herself, had she? she thought further. She still wore the slate-blue scrubs she preferred for work, and she still bound her dark-brown hair in a tidy braid. But then, why fix it if it wasn't broken, right?

"Excuse me, but I've been waiting for more than a half hour now," a young woman told Rita as she leaned over the counter of the nurses' station. She seemed to be checking the desk to make sure there were no extra doctors hiding there. "How much longer will it be until I can see someone?"

Rita offered up a halfhearted smile. "It shouldn't be too much longer, I wouldn't think," she said, knowing she was being optimistic, but feeling hopeful all the same. "This flu that's going around has hit everyone hard. We're even short a doctor this morning because of it."

Plus, they were understandably obligated to take the most serious cases first. With a slight fever and cough, and no family doctor, this woman was in for a wait.

Now, too, they were expecting an ambulance, whose arrival they had been alerted to only moments ago. A homeless man had gone into cardiac arrest not far from the hospital. Rita had already notified the coronary care unit, and they were sending down their best—Dr. Matthew Grayson, who was something of a legend around Boston General.

Truth be told, his legendary status wasn't due entirely to his talent as a heart surgeon. No, part of his status was less legend-like than it was fairy-tale-like. Dr. Grayson definitely resembled a certain fairy-tale character—the Beast from *Beauty and the Beast*. It wasn't just because of his attitude, either, though certainly that had been described as beastly by more than one CCU nurse. One would think that as a result of working in the unit herself, Rita would have more than a nodding acquaintance with Dr. Grayson. But she didn't think anyone in the CCU—or at Boston General for that matter—had any kind of acquaintance with the man.

Although Rita had never been put off by Dr. Grayson the way many were, she could see why others might find him difficult. At times he was gruff to the extreme. Even in his best mood, he was standoffish. His beastliness was only enhanced by the scars on the left side of his face and neck. She didn't know what had caused those scars—Dr. Grayson never mentioned them, and neither did anyone else if they knew what was good for them—but whatever it had been had done a thorough job in marking him. It was obvious that he'd had cosmetic surgery, but even plastic surgeons couldn't work miracles. Dr. Grayson, she was sure, would remain scarred for life.

But whether he truly was a beast, Rita couldn't say. Yes, he could be intimidating, but he was a dedicated professional who saved scores of lives. Rita admired and respected his skill as a surgeon, and she figured he probably had a reason for his gruffness. In any event, he'd never turned that attitude on her. Come to think of it, he pretty much steered clear of her, which was just fine with her.

Besides, it took a lot more than scars and a bad mood to intimidate Rita Barone. The second-youngest of eight children from a celebrated Boston family, she'd had no choice but to learn early on to take care of herself and not let things get to her. She'd grown up with four rough-and-tumble older brothers who'd suffered every manner of injury known to humankind, not to mention their own forms of beastly behavior, especially when puberty struck them.

As if conjured by the thought, Dr. Matthew Grayson himself appeared then, rushing toward the nurses' station. His white coat flapped behind him over dark trousers, a white shirt and a discreetly patterned necktie in varying shades of blue.

"Has our cardiac arrest arrived yet?" he demanded without so much as a hello as he came to a stop behind Rita.

"Any time now," she told him.

Really, she thought, considering him, if it weren't for the scars on his face, he'd be an extremely handsome man. Standing at about six-foot-three, he towered over Rita, something she wasn't accustomed to at five-eight herself. Add to that impressive height his solid, athletic build, his dreamy green eyes and his chestnut hair with its golden highlights, not to mention the perfectly tailored, very expensive dark suits he generally opted for, and you had the makings of a Hollywood movie star. Only the scars marred his perfection.

Then again, she thought further, in some ways those scars almost added to his allure. They kept his exquisite good looks from being *too* exquisite, and somehow made him seem more human.

Of course, at the moment, he seemed more godlike, as he towered over her. Rita fought the urge to stand up, though that scarcely would have made a difference, thanks to the disparity in their heights. Instead, she remained seated, as if she were completely unaffected by his near-ness. And she was—except for the way her heart rate seemed to have quadrupled the moment she saw him strid-ing toward her.

But then, what else was her heart supposed to do? she wondered. They were expecting a cardiac arrest any mo-ment, and Dr. Grayson had already surged into action in anticipation. It was normal that she be surging, too, albeit in *other* ways. Ways that had nothing to do with the good doctor's presence. Especially once she heard the siren out-side announcing the arrival of the ambulance. She leapt up from her chair and circled the nurses' station with Dr. Gray-son right on her heels.

In a flurry of motion and clamor, the paramedics wheeled in an elderly man who was screaming and keening and flailing his arms about. He was filthy, Rita saw as she ap-proached, hurrying her stride to match the paramedics' as she directed them to an examining room, and he was clearly terrified. As she strode alongside him, instinctively she reached for the man's hand and held it, then winced a bit when he squeezed tightly enough to hurt her. He was ob-viously much stronger than he looked.

"It's okay," she told him as they came to a halt in a small room. "You're going to be all right." She didn't know if that was true, but she wasn't about to cite heart-attack survival statistics for him right now. "You've got the best here to help you," she said further. "We'll take good care of you."

The man stopped trying to strike the paramedics then, and he stopped shouting. When he turned to look at Rita, he was breathing rapidly and raggedly, and his pale-blue eyes were filled with fear.

"Who—who're you?" he gasped. Then he grimaced in pain.

"My name is Rita," she said soothingly, stroking her other hand over the one he had wrapped so fiercely around hers. As discreetly as she could, she took his pulse, not wanting to alarm him again. It wasn't quite as erratic as she would have thought under the circumstances, but it was still thready.

"You—the—doc?" the man asked with some difficulty, his voice raspy, his breathing becoming more labored.

"No, I'm a nurse," Rita told him as she noted the activity surrounding them. It looked as if half the staff was in the tiny room, tending to the man, even though she knew it was only a fraction of those working this morning. "But there's a doctor here," she said further. "You're in the emergency room of Boston General, and you're having a heart attack. I'm going to take your blood pressure now," she then added. When he recoiled and opened his mouth to shout again, she hastily, but very calmly, added, "It won't hurt, I promise. But you need to let us check you out, to see how you're doing."

"We've stabilized him," one of the paramedics said from the other side of the gurney, "but he's not out of the woods yet. Not by a long shot."

Rita threw the man a censuring look. The last thing this guy needed to hear was that he was still in danger.

"Am I—" He grimaced again, groaning. "Am I—gonna—die?" he demanded.

"No," Rita said firmly, gritting her teeth at the paramedic, who just shrugged off her reproach. "You're going to be fine. What's your name?" she asked the old man.

He gazed at her warily for a moment, still clearly frightened, then, evidently deciding she was okay, he told her weakly, "Joe."

"Do you have any family, Joe?" she asked as the others were working to monitor him, hooking him up to oxygen and an EKG. He fought the mask at first, but Rita soothed him, promising him it was for his own good and that it would only be temporary. "Is there anyone we can call who might make you feel more comfortable?" she asked again.

He shook his head, took another indifferent swipe at the oxygen mask, then surrendered to it. "No. No family," he told her, sounding even weaker than he had before. After a small hesitation, he added, "But—but you kinda—" He expelled a sound of pain, then grabbed her hand again with a brutal grip. "You," he tried again, "you—make me feel—more comfortable."

Rita smiled again, flexing her fingers against the force of his grasp. "Well, then, Joe, I'll just stay right here with you. How will that be?"

He nodded faintly. "That'd be good. Don't—go nowhere."

"I won't," she promised him.

"And later," he said, his voice quavering as he spoke, "after—after they's—done with me, if I—if I make it through—don't—go nowhere then, neither."

Rita patted his hand gently. "This is where I work, Joe. And you know, sometimes I feel like I never leave."

That roused a brief, if feeble, grin from him in response, but he was clearly growing weaker now. She sent up a silent prayer that he would be all right. She knew nothing about him except that he had no home and no family and that his name was Joe. But he was obviously a fighter—and a survivor—and she had no choice but to admire that. Surely he'd survive this, too.

"This is Dr. Grayson," Rita told him, nodding her head toward the surgeon who now stood on the other side of the gurney. "He'll be looking at you here in a minute. He's very good. The absolute best."

When she looked up, she saw that Dr. Grayson was studying her with much consideration, as if he wanted to ask her something, and she opened her mouth to ask what. But Joe began thrashing and screaming then, and thinking he must be in pain, Rita glanced back down to tend to him. But it obviously wasn't pain that was causing his reaction. He was looking right at Dr. Grayson and had somehow managed to lift his hand to point at the scars on the other man's face.

"Don't let 'im—come near me," Joe said with much agitation. "He—he ain't—no man. He's a—monster."

Dr. Grayson simply ignored the comment and reached toward Joe. Joe, however, shoved his hand away before the doctor could touch him, and began to thrash even more.

"Git 'im—away from me! Git 'im away!"

"Joe, please," Rita tried again.

But the old man wouldn't be calmed. "His face!" he cried, pointing at Dr. Grayson. "He's like one a'them—one a'them gargoyles on—St. Michael's. They—come after me sometimes—in my—in my dreams. To take me—to hell. They's monsters! Git 'im away!"

"Joe, it's all right," Rita said firmly, grabbing his arms and holding them at his sides. "Dr. Grayson is here to help you. He's an excellent surgeon and a wonderful man. No one is going to hurt you," she said even more forcefully. "I won't let anyone hurt you, I promise. I'm right here, and I won't let anyone hurt you."

For whatever reason, her vows reassured him. Or maybe it was just that he was too weak and in too much pain to fight anymore. Rita gave up trying to be a nurse then and let the other RNs tend to Joe's medical needs. Instead, she picked up the man's hand once more and held it tightly, and murmured soothing words about how he was going to be just fine because he had Dr. Matthew Grayson to take care of him.

And he would be fine, Rita told herself, feeling strangely attached to the old man for some reason. Because he did have Dr. Matthew Grayson to look after him.

Who wouldn't be fine with someone like that to watch over him?

One

***

The coronary care unit at Boston General in the trendy North End was quiet for a Friday at dinnertime—no doubt the rowdy April weather outside was keeping many visitors at home—which meant that Rita Barone actually found five full minutes to steal away from the nurses' station for a cup of bad coffee from the vending machine in the CCU waiting room. Coffee—even bad coffee—was her only hope to get her through the evening shift, one she hadn't worked in months. After three years at Boston General, she had finally landed regular hours in the day shift, and only had to pull night hours now to cover for friends, like tonight, or to pick up extra Christmas money. Not that extra Christmas money was generally a big deal, since the Barones of Boston were *never* strapped for cash. But Rita was the kind of woman who liked to rest on her own laurels, and not the family's, so she rarely, if ever, took advantage of the Barone family's very fat coffers.

Three years, she reflected again as she watched the vending machine spit its dark-brown brew into a paper container that was in no way large enough to qualify for a respectable cup of coffee. In fact, it had been three years to the day today, she realized further. She had begun working at Boston General as a student nurse exactly two months before her June graduation from Boston University, and exactly one month following her twenty-second birthday. Now, at twenty-five, here she was celebrating her anniversary by being back on the evening shift.

She glanced down at her watch, then shook her head morosely. She'd only started two hours ago, and already she was hitting the caffeine. The six remaining hours had never seemed like such a long, looming stretch of time.

She kept a close eye on the too-full cup of coffee as she made her way back to the nurses' station, then returned to her seat and set the hot brew to the side to cool a bit. Absently, she tucked a stray strand of dark-brown hair back into the thick French braid that fell to the base of her neck, then brushed at a stain of indistinguishable origin on the pants of her slate-blue scrubs. It wasn't until she was reaching for a patient chart that she saw the small white package tucked sideways into her note slot on the desk.

And she battled a wave of apprehension that shimmied down her spine when she saw it.

It hadn't been there when she'd gone for her coffee, because she'd had to reach into her mail slot to grab some of the spare change she always left there for the vending machines. So whoever had left it had done so just now, while she was gone. It was a small square box wrapped in white glossy paper, tied with a gold ribbon, obviously a gift. But instead of being delighted by such a surprise, Rita went cold inside. This was the third time she'd found a gift in her note slot wrapped in exactly this way. As always, when she looked for a note to accompany the gift, she didn't find one. And, as always, that bothered her. A lot.

Okay, she admitted, she *had* been delighted the first time such a gift had shown up, on Valentine's Day, two months ago—for all of a few hours. When she'd returned from lunch that day and found a tiny present tucked into her note slot, she'd been reluctantly enchanted, especially when she found that there was no note accompanying the gift to explain its presence. She'd been even more enchanted when she'd opened the box to find a small pin inside. It was a pewter heart, not much bigger than a postage stamp, wrapped diagonally with a gold Band-Aid. She'd thought it an appropriate gift for a cardiology nurse, and had immediately pinned the heart to the breast pocket of her scrubs, just above her name tag. Then she'd waited for the giver to come forward and identify him- or herself, and his or her reason for the gesture.

Of course, since the occasion on that first gift's appearance was Valentine's Day, her co-workers had proposed that Rita must have a secret admirer. Rita, naturally, had considered such a suggestion ridiculous. Grown men didn't have secret crushes on grown women—not emotionally sound grown men, anyway. But her fellow nurses had insisted, and it hadn't been long before the rumor mill at Boston General—an astoundingly active one—was churning out a story about Rita Barone's secret admirer.

Who could it be? everyone wondered. One of the handsome new interns? A co-worker who was too shy to make his affections known? A former patient who felt his life had been saved by the lovely, dark-eyed, dark-haired cardiology nurse?

Although a number of people had remarked on the pin that day, none had claimed to be the one who gave it to Rita. Nor had any of her co-workers seen anyone put the gift in her note slot. So Rita began to wear the pin daily, certain that eventually someone would admit to having given it to her. Perhaps there was supposed to have been a card, but it had got lost somehow. Perhaps someone simply wanted to tease her a bit by leaving her curious for a few days before identifying himself as the giver. Perhaps the person was shy, in which case that shyness might be assuaged if the person saw her wearing the gift.

But in spite of Rita continually wearing the pin, and in spite of the number of comments she received about it, no one ever came forward.

The second gift had arrived in her note slot last month, on her birthday. Again, it had been wrapped in white, glossy paper with a gold ribbon, and again, it had appeared without a card or note. When Rita had opened that one, hoping perhaps it might offer some clue as to the identity of its giver, she had found inside an inexpensive silver charm bracelet with a dozen delicate little charms related to the nursing field. She'd been reluctantly pleased by it, too, but hadn't quite been able to halt the feeling of foreboding that had accompanied her pleasure.

She'd told herself her apprehension was silly, that obviously she *did* have a secret admirer—and hey, why was that such a bad thing? Then she'd donned the charm bracelet, as well, hoping again to "out" the giver.

But again, no one came forth to claim the identity of Rita Barone's secret admirer. No one came forth for any reason at all.

Now, as she eyed this latest gift with a mixture of hesitant pleasure and growing dread, she lifted her right hand to stroke the bandaged heart pin fastened, as it always was, on the pocket of her scrubs. When she did, the charm bracelet clinked merrily on her right wrist.

Now the mysterious giver had struck again, had left her

a third gift—on the third anniversary of her having started work at Boston General.

Whoever it was, she realized then, was commemorating special occasions and events—first Valentine's Day, then her birthday, and now the anniversary of her first day at work. It must be someone who worked at the hospital, she thought. And it must be a secret admirer—for lack of a better ID. There were too many romantic overtones for it not to be. Still, she couldn't begin to imagine who might be leaving her gifts like this. She'd noticed not one hint of interest from anyone of the opposite sex, absolutely no clue that there was a man out there who regarded her as anything more than another human being who inhabited the same planet. Not at work, and not anywhere else, either.

Not unless she was overlooking any hints and clues a man might be giving out, which she supposed was possible, since she'd really never been much interested in the opposite sex. Her sisters Gina and Maria often told her she was so focused on her work that she was missing out on everything else life had to offer, including romance.

Of course, Rita didn't necessarily disagree with that. Her work *was* very important to her. More important, she admitted, than anything else. Except for family, of course. The Barones were a close-knit bunch, and family would always come first for all of them. But Rita had never wanted to be anything but a nurse, ever since she was a child, and the job gave her more satisfaction and fulfillment than she could imagine receiving anywhere else. She helped save lives here at the hospital. What could possibly be more important than that?

Well, there was saving her own life, Gina would always argue when Rita pointed that out, seeing as how Rita didn't much have one outside work. And there was living her life, Maria would chime in, the one outside work, anyway.

Whenever her sisters offered their opinions in such a way, Rita would blithely remind them that her work *was* her life, and she enjoyed it very much, thanks. And she truly did believe it was enough. She had a full, and very satisfying, life without having to wade through all the politics and games of a romantic relationship—especially a workplace romance.

Still, she thought now as she gingerly fingered the third little white package, it would be nice to discover who was leaving the gifts for her. If nothing else, she could rest easy knowing there was nothing more to it than someone having a bit of fun. Because she just couldn't quite shake the sensation that there was something a bit sinister about all this anonymous gift-giving, even if the gifts in question had been totally benign.

Rita checked one more time to see if there was a card or note to accompany the gift but, not surprisingly, she found none. So, inhaling a deep breath, she tucked her finger under the gold ribbon and slowly slid it off. Then she carefully peeled back the white paper. Just as it had been with the previous two gifts, the box was plain and white, too, with no markings that might identify where the gift had been purchased. Placing it cautiously on the desk, Rita lifted the lid, then pushed aside a fold of tissue paper.

"Oh, my," she said softly, reverently, when she saw what was inside. A small, cut-crystal heart winked merrily at her from its cushion of tissue in the box, shattering the harsh fluorescent overhead light into a billion kaleidoscopic colors. It was meant, she supposed, to be a paperweight. Somehow, though, it was much too beautiful for so functional a purpose.

A crystal heart, she remarked again. Was it a symbol of what she did for a living, caring for a fragile organ? Or a symbol of the giver's fragile feelings for her? And how would she ever know if the giver never came forward? And why wouldn't he? It had been two months since that first gift had appeared. Surely, by now, he was ready to make himself known. Unless…

Unless his intentions were less than honorable.

"Have you nothing better to do with your time, Ms. Barone, than enjoy an extended coffee break?"

Rita jumped at the gruffly offered question, not so much because of the question itself—unfair as it was—but because the voice belonged to Dr. Matthew Grayson. In addition to his medical skills, he was renowned for his no-nonsense approach to his work.

And also because of his complete intolerance for anything bordering on fun.

Tall, dark and brooding, that was Dr. Grayson. All the nurses and other doctors thought so. And most steered clear of him whenever they could, because they didn't want to get caught in the storm swirling in the dark clouds that always seemed to surround him. Rita, though, had always thought him rather intriguing. Nobody was born grouchy and aloof, she reasoned. Something had to happen in a person's life to make him that way. And Rita couldn't help wondering what had happened in Matthew Grayson's.

She also couldn't help wondering if it had anything to do with the scars he bore on his left cheek and neck. The worst of them were a trio of nearly straight lines that ran from his cheekbone to his jaw—three parallel stripes, roughly a half inch apart and three inches in length.

Automatically she slammed the lid back down on the box she had just opened. For some reason, she didn't want Dr. Grayson to know about her secret admirer—if admiring was indeed what was behind the mysterious gifts. As discreetly as she could, she slid the box back into her note slot, tossed the white wrapping paper and gold ribbon into the wastebasket beneath her desk, and then turned in her chair to face him.

Big mistake, she realized immediately. Because being seated while he was standing left Rita gazing at a part of Dr. Grayson she really shouldn't be gazing at.

"Dr. Grayson," she said as she abruptly stood, telling herself she was only imagining the breathless quality her voice seemed to have suddenly adopted. "I didn't hear you coming."

"Obviously," he replied wryly.

"And I wasn't enjoying a coffee break," she assured him.

He gazed pointedly at the cup sitting before her chair.

"Okay, yes, I *was* having coffee," she conceded. "But I *wasn't* enjoying it. It's from the vending machine," she added meaningfully.

Dr. Grayson, however, evidently didn't catch her meaning, because he only continued to scowl at her. Granted, it was kind of a handsome scowl, what with those dreamy green eyes and that full, luscious-looking mouth, but it was a scowl nonetheless. So Rita countered with the most dazzling smile she could conjure from her ample arsenal. She knew it made him uncomfortable to be smiled at. Probably, she thought, because he didn't know how to smile back. In fact, she'd never seen him smile. And, true to her supposition—and his own personality—Dr. Grayson only deepened his scowl. So Rita smiled even more dazzlingly, this time batting her eyelashes playfully.

There, she thought triumphantly. Take *that,* Dr. Grayson.

But instead of being immobilized by her mischievous warfare, Dr. Grayson only looked more ferocious. So, with an imperceptible sigh, Rita surrendered.

Point to Dr. Grayson.

"Rita," he said in a tone of voice that indicated he

wanted to start all over again and pretend the last few moments hadn't happened, which was fine with her, "we've just admitted a new patient who will be arriving in CCU shortly, a Mr. Harold Asgaard. He's scheduled for surgery at seven in the morning, but I want him monitored closely throughout the evening and all through the night."

Somehow, Rita refrained from a salute. Still, she dutifully replied, "Yes, sir. I'll see to it."

"Good."

"Anything else?" she asked when he added nothing more. She found it odd that he'd sought her out just to tell her to closely monitor a patient who was scheduled for surgery in the morning. That was standard operating procedure in CCU.

Dr. Grayson dropped his gaze to the chart he held in one hand, began scanning it, then shook his head. "No, I think that's all for now. You're on evening shift tonight?" he asked, stating the obvious, still scanning the chart, as if he were uncomfortable meeting her gaze.

"Um, yes," Rita replied in light of the obvious.

"Covering for Nancy?"

"Rosemary, actually," Rita said. "Her great-grandmother's one-hundredth birthday party is tonight, so she and I traded off today. Nancy's left the unit. She transferred to pediatrics last week."

Dr. Grayson nodded, as if just now remembering, and continued to scan the chart. Continued to avoid Rita's gaze. "That's right," he said absently. "I'd forgotten."

Rita eyed him suspiciously. It wasn't like Matthew Grayson to forget things. And it wasn't like him to avoid anyone's gaze. What was up with him today? He seemed a little…off.

"Is everything okay, Dr. Grayson?" she asked before thinking. "You don't seem like yourself."

His gaze shot back up to meet hers, and only then did Rita realize how familiarly she had spoken to him. Boston General didn't have rules against such behavior, but Dr. Grayson *did*. And everyone knew it, because he'd made it clear over the years that he was *not* the kind of person who spoke about personal things. But Rita couldn't help it. It was in her nature. Family matters were a big deal with the Barones, and were generally discussed quite candidly.

Still, she should have known better with Dr. Grayson. She didn't know what she was thinking to have asked him such a question and offered such a remark about his well-being.

"And who do I seem like, Rita?" he asked coolly.

"Uh, no one in particular. Just…you know…not yourself."

"And how does myself usually seem?" he asked further.

"Uh… I, uh… What I meant was… It's just that…" Great. Now she'd done it. How did one get oneself out of a painted corner without messing up one's shoes? she wondered.

"Yes, Rita, everything is fine," Dr. Grayson finally interjected before she gave herself enough rope for a self-inflicted hanging. And in doing so, he simultaneously put her out of her misery, and put her back up in the process. "Not that that's any of your concern," he added sharply.

Another point to the beastly Dr. Grayson, Rita thought.

She bit her lower lip to keep in a tart retort. Instead, she nodded silently and glanced momentarily away. But when she looked his way again, she noticed his eyes weren't meeting hers, though his attention was lingering on her face. More specifically, on her mouth, she realized. He was noticing how she was anxiously biting her lip and…

…and probably thinking her the worst kind of neurotic. Immediately, she ceased her fretting and forced herself to attention. "I'm sorry," she said, though even she couldn't detect a trace of apology in her voice. "I didn't mean to pry."

"Didn't you?" he asked.

She shook her head, knowing she spoke the truth. Why would she want to pry into Matthew Grayson's life? Just because she found his seemingly inexplicable gruffness intriguing? Just because he had such dreamy green eyes? Just because he seemed to be as dedicated to his work as Rita was to hers? Just because he had such dreamy green eyes? Just because she'd been wondering since the day she started working in CCU what his story was? Just because he had such dreamy green eyes? Just because she wished she could work up the nerve to ask him about those scars on his face and neck?

And had she mentioned his dreamy green eyes?

Get a grip, Rita, she told herself. This was Matthew Grayson, MD, whose green eyes she found so dreamy. He was a distinguished cardiac surgeon and an eminent curmudgeon, probably almost ten years her senior and too serious by half. He wasn't the kind of man she should be wondering about in *any* way. He wasn't her type at all.

Not that she had a type, she quickly reminded herself. But if she did have a type, it wouldn't be Matthew Grayson, MD.

Even if he did have dreamy green eyes.

"No, I didn't," she said, recalling now that he had asked a question. "I didn't mean to pry. I was just a little concerned, that's all."

Dr. Grayson studied her for a moment more, long enough to make Rita think he was wondering something about her, too. Then, in a brisk, that-will-be-all kind of voice, he assured her, "You needn't be concerned about me." Before

she had a chance to comment further, he spun on his heel
and walked away.

Point three to the Beast.

Rita was a Barone, though, and Barones always got in
the last word, no matter how many points behind they were.
Always. So, quietly enough that he couldn't hear, and to
his retreating back, she said, "Trust me, Dr. Grayson, when
I say that I *won't* be concerned about you. Ever."

Point to the Barone. Finally.

Then Rita returned to both her chair and her work. Still
not feeling as if that last word was quite enough, however,
she glanced back up in time to see Dr. Grayson's imposing
figure disappearing around the corner at the end of the corridor. And she fired off another last word to punctuate the
others.

"Beast," she said.

For some reason, though, it didn't make her feel any
better.

Matthew Grayson managed—barely—to make it back to
his office in the medical towers adjoining Boston General
before his knees finally collapsed beneath him. He stag-
gered over to his desk and toppled into the leather chair
behind it, then inhaled a deep, ragged breath in the hopes
that it might quell the rapid-fire banging of his heart. Then
he called himself every kind of fool.

Rita Barone had come *this* close to catching him this
time. When he'd seen her leave the nurses' station, he'd
thought she was taking a longer break than a few short
minutes, so he hadn't been in any hurry to slip the little
package from the pocket of his jacket into her mail slot.
Plus, he'd had to wait for another nurse and a visitor to
conclude their conversation near the nurses' station and
walk off before he could even approach. He couldn't risk

anyone seeing him anywhere near Rita's station when he did what he had to do.

He'd only just managed to leave the gift and steal away before she'd returned. Lucky for him she'd been entirely focused on not spilling her coffee as she'd walked down the corridor. Had she glanced up, even for a second, she would have seen him standing there, then would have found the gift after he left, and then would have had no trouble deducing who had been leaving her mysterious presents for the past two months.

And damned if Matthew didn't feel like the biggest buffoon on the planet for leaving those mysterious presents. Here he was, a thirty-three-year-old man, one of the most noted surgeons in New England, and a member of one of Boston's most illustrious families, and he was behaving like a goofy junior-high-school kid, leaving secret gifts in the locker of the girl he liked. What in God's name had reduced him to such behavior?

Well, of course, he knew that. And he felt like an even bigger buffoon admitting it. It was the simple presence of Rita Barone in the coronary care unit at Boston General. The "beastly" Dr. Grayson—yes, he knew quite well what his nickname was around the hospital; he had ears, after all—had a crush on one of the nurses. And not just any nurse, but a nurse who was young and pretty and vivacious. A nurse who would surely be shocked and repulsed if she ever found out the identity of her secret admirer.

Talk about your Beauty and the Beast scenarios. Without even meaning to, Matthew had reduced himself to a cliché.

Gingerly, he lifted his hand to his left cheek, tracing his index finger over the scars that even the most talented plastic surgeons and the most sophisticated cosmetic surgical techniques couldn't erase. The deepest of the wounds had gone straight down to the bone. Well, the deepest of the physical wounds, at any rate. Over the past twenty-three years, Matthew had undergone more surgery for his face than he cared to think about. Really, he supposed he looked pretty good, considering the viciousness of the attack and the depth of the damage. Physically, any scarring that was left was relatively superficial. Emotionally, however…

Well. Those injuries had gone straight down *into* the bone, and in many ways, had been even more damaging than the physical ones. Nor were they as repairable. Although he knew no one was perfect, Matthew was imperfect in ways that most people were not. He couldn't imagine someone like Rita Barone—someone who *was* very nearly perfect, at least in his eyes—ever wanting to get any closer to him than she had to.

He propped his elbows on his desk, closed his eyes, and buried his face in his hands, hoping that by doing so, he might be able to think about something else, visualize something other than Rita's dark, soulful eyes and her lush mouth. But he couldn't stop replaying the image of her nibbling her lip the way she had, and he couldn't halt the heat that swept through him when he remembered it. He could still hear the sound of her soft sigh and her reverently whispered "Oh, my" as she opened the box with the crystal heart, and that, too, filled him with a strange sort of warmth unlike anything he had ever felt before.

She had liked her gift, he realized, relief coursing through him like a slowly thawing springtime stream. And she had been wearing the bracelet and pin, too, just as she had worn them at work every day since he'd left them for her. Something about that gladdened Matthew, as if there was a little part of him she kept with her every day, even if she didn't realize it herself.

Surely, he thought further, there was something wrong

with him, finding a guilty sort of pleasure in a secret he was sharing with no one.

No, he immediately corrected himself, dropping his hands from his face to place them resolutely on his desk. He did *not* have a crush on Rita Barone. It wasn't that at all. He focused his gaze on the opposite wall of his office, the one hung with his degrees and awards and commendations. He wasn't the kind of man to have crushes. He was far too pragmatic and accomplished.

He admired Rita Barone, he told himself, that was all. Admired her on a professional level, and nothing more. Surely there was nothing wrong with admiring a co-worker. Nor was there anything wrong with being unable to verbally articulate that admiration. There were plenty of people who were uncomfortable expressing such sentiments. Matthew had never been one for the touchy-feely sharing of emotions—none of the Graysons were—and God knew he wasn't about to start now.

He admired Rita Barone, he told himself again, more adamantly this time. He respected her dedication to her work, and he appreciated her ability to relate to patients in a kind and caring fashion.

Take last February, with a homeless man named Joe. Rita had calmed the man's fears, and stayed by his side throughout his open-heart surgery. Because of her, the old man had made a total recovery.

Matthew had been amazed by her kindness and nurturing during that time. He'd envied her then—and still did—the gift she had for relating to and sympathizing with others, two things he'd never been able to master himself. Of course, there was a reason for that, but it didn't keep Matthew from feeling diminished in that regard. As he'd watched Rita interact with Joe, Matthew had been touched on a level where he'd never felt anything before.

Back in February, he'd wanted to do something to let Rita know how much he had appreciated her help with Joe. Since he was uncomfortable vocalizing such things, he'd decided to leave some small token of his gratitude in her mail slot instead. He'd seen the bandaged heart pin in the hospital gift shop, and he'd thought it would make an appropriate gift. He'd written a note of thanks to leave with it, but the day had been so hectic, he'd forgotten to include it. He'd also forgotten that the day in question was Valentine's Day.

It was only later, when he began to hear the rumors about Rita Barone's secret admirer that he realized what he had done. The last thing he'd wanted to do at that point was identify himself and risk being labeled Rita's secret admirer by the hospital grapevine. That would have only led to teasing, and Matthew *hated* to be teased. There was a reason for that, too, but no one would have cared. All he'd known then was that he couldn't let himself be fingered as Rita Barone's secret admirer. So he'd tossed the note in the garbage and kept his mouth shut.

Of course, that didn't explain why he'd felt compelled to leave her another gift last month, on her birthday, or a third gift this evening, on the anniversary of her start at Boston General. Hell, it didn't explain why he even knew those dates. And it certainly didn't explain why he'd deliberately made sure those gifts were given anonymously. What did explain that, Matthew thought now, was...

Ah, dammit. He didn't have an explanation for it.

Sure, you do, he told himself sarcastically. *You admire her. On a professional level. There's nothing more to it than that. Even if she does have the kind of dark, soulful eyes a man could get lost in forever and never find his way back.*

Oh, stop it, Matthew commanded himself. *You're getting maudlin in your old age.*

And old was often how he felt around Rita Barone. Old and scarred and beastly.

Enough! he shouted inwardly. He had plenty to occupy his mind at the moment other than thoughts of a certain dark-eyed, dark-haired nurse that made him feel foolish. He had surgery scheduled early tomorrow morning, and he had yet to make his final rounds. Rita Barone was the last thing he should be thinking about. She was his co-worker, nothing more. And she was too young and spirited and beautiful to be interested in someone old and scarred and beastly.

And even if there was the potential for something to develop between them—which was highly unlikely—her family was the nouveau riche Barone clan, while his own was old-money Bostonian. The Graysons had come over on the *Mayflower,* for God's sake, and they never let anyone forget it. The Barones, on the other hand, had come over in steerage. They came from humble beginnings and had only recently made their fortune, and in the Italian ice-cream business, of all things. Talk about your frivolous pursuits. The Graysons, by and large, were financiers. Much more respectable work—at least, as far as the elder Graysons were concerned.

No, there was no way his parents would ever approve of a Grayson–Barone merger, and they'd make things very difficult for Matthew—and for Rita, too. Especially after the sordid, scandalous stories that had been splashed across the tabloids last month about one of Rita's sisters. He vaguely remembered something about suggestive photos better suited to men's magazines than respectable newspapers. Not that the tabloids were in any way respectable. But they were read. Doubtless the photos had never been meant for public consumption, but consumed by the public they had been—rabidly. And although the old-money Bostonians might turn their noses up at scandal and gossip, it certainly didn't keep them from gossiping about scandal. There was no way Matthew's mother would let any of the Barones come near her family or her home.

Not that it mattered. There were just too many things that didn't mesh between Matthew and Rita for there to be anything to worry about, he told himself again. Therefore, he wouldn't worry about it.

And he wouldn't think about her dark, soulful eyes.

Two

Rita was absolutely beat when she finally got home just after midnight. Not surprisingly, the brownstone on Paul Revere Way looked dark and quiet as she climbed the handful of steps to the front door and unlocked it. Her older sister Gina had moved out last month, after marrying Flint Kingman, and Rita and Maria were still trying to find a suitable tenant for the empty top-floor apartment. And her younger sister Maria was doubtless just out, as she so often seemed to be these days.

In fact, Maria had been going out way more often than usual lately, Rita reflected as she locked the door behind herself. Which was surprising, because Maria didn't have a steady boyfriend, or much of a social life outside of her work managing the original Baronessa Gelateria on Hanover Street. She used to be home as often as Rita was. But for the past couple of months she'd been out quite a lot, something that suggested there might be someone special in her life. But Maria hadn't mentioned meeting anyone, and Rita certainly hadn't seen her with anyone out of the ordinary.

As she stepped into the foyer of the brownstone, she realized immediately that she was indeed alone. The first floor of the four-story brick building served as a kind of community living room for the sisters, and tended to be a place of congregation, regardless of the hour. With its hardwood floors and leafy plants and beige furnishings and powder-blue accents in the form of pillows and such, the first floor of the brownstone was inviting in a comfy, elegant kind of way that made people want to linger. At the moment, though, it was empty, and not so much as a discarded jacket or pair of shoes indicated that anyone had been home anytime recently.

Rita had, as she always did in the afternoons following her shift, walked home tonight, unconcerned about her safety because the streets of Boston's North End were always well populated on a Friday night, even in a light drizzle, as there was tonight. Now she shrugged off her raincoat and ran her fingers through her damp, dark bangs, then forsook the elevator to make her way up the stairs to her third-floor apartment. Once inside, she hung her coat on the rack by the door and went straight to her kitchen to brew herself a cup of chamomile tea. She wasn't normally a night owl, but she was still too wound up from her shift to go to bed just yet. So, dipping her teabag in and out of her mug, she moved to the bathroom for a long, hot soak in a tub full of lavender-scented water.

It was going on one-thirty, and she was about to turn off her bedside lamp, when she heard Maria coming in downstairs. Pushing back the covers, Rita climbed out of bed and padded barefoot to her front door, waiting until she knew for sure that her sister was alone before opening it.

It wasn't so much that she didn't want to interrupt anything Maria might be doing with the potential someone special in her life that she didn't seem to want to tell anyone about, but Rita didn't want anyone else to catch her in her neon-pink pajamas decorated with ice-cream desserts, which she'd fallen in love with at the store and thought appropriate for a Barone. But she detected no footsteps other than Maria's on the stairs, so she stepped out of her apartment, peeked over the stair rail and called down to her sister.

"Hey, you," she said. "Where have you been?"

At the summons, Maria looked up over the stair rail two floors below and smiled. Her dark hair fell just below her shoulders, and her dark eyes twinkled merrily, even in the scant stairwell light. "Hi," she called softly out of habit, even though there was no one else in the building to disturb anymore. But instead of answering Rita's question, she asked one of her own. "What are you doing up so late?"

Rita hesitated a moment before telling her sister, "I got another anonymous gift at work tonight."

Immediately Maria's smile fell. "That's what? Three now?"

Rita nodded.

"And you still have no idea who's leaving them?"

Now Rita shook her head. "And no idea why."

"Let me drop my purse and shoes in my apartment," Maria said, "and I'll be right up."

Rita murmured her thanks and returned to her own apartment, leaving her door open so that her sister could come inside. A few moments later Maria arrived, still dressed in her Friday-night outfit of black capri pants and sapphire-blue silk shirt. The combination was striking with her dark good looks, and Rita, who was hopelessly fashion-challenged, made a mental note to copy a similar outfit the next time she went out. Then she wondered why she was bothering to make such a mental note, seeing as she never went out anyway.

She sighed fitfully as Maria took her seat on the over-stuffed chintz sofa opposite the overstuffed chintz chair Rita occupied herself. Her decorating sense was no better than her fashion sense, so she'd copied the room down to every detail from a photograph in a magazine. Between the chintz furniture and the lace curtains, and the hooked floral rugs on the hardwood floor, she'd managed to capture an English-country-cottage look fairly well, right down to the dried flower wreaths and watercolor landscapes on the cream-colored walls. Usually, this room soothed Rita. Tonight, though, she just felt edgy.

"You didn't see who left it?" Maria asked without preamble.

Again Rita shook her head. "And it's really starting to creep me out, Maria. I mean, why would he leave gifts without letting me know who he is?"

"What do your instincts tell you?" Maria asked.

Rita thought about that for a moment. "I don't know," she said honestly. "Part of me feels like whoever is doing it is doing it because he's shy and is afraid I might rebuff him."

"How does the other part of you feel?"

Rita met her sister's gaze levelly now. "Like maybe he's not shy. Like maybe he's a—" She couldn't even say the word aloud.

"A stalker?" Maria asked, voicing the very word Rita had hoped so much to avoid. Just like that, a cold shudder went scurrying right down her spine.

"Yeah," she said. "Like maybe he's...one of those."

Maria looked doubtful. "I don't know," she said. "Maybe I'm being naive, but I bet you do just have some kind of secret admirer at the hospital. I mean, don't stalkers usually strike closer to home? And don't they inspire terror? What was the gift this time? Unless it was a decapitated pet or a dismembered Barbie doll or something, you're probably fine."

Rita rose from the sofa and went to retrieve the square white box from her purse, then took it to Maria and placed it in her palm.

"Too small to be a decapitated pet," her sister quipped. "Unless you've been keeping goldfish you haven't told me about. Just promise me there's not a severed Barbie hand in there."

"Maria," Rita said pleadingly.

"All right, all right. Enough with the sick jokes. I was just trying to make you feel better."

"Talk of headless animals and doll parts is *not* making me feel better," Rita told her.

"I apologize. It's late," her sister said by way of an explanation. Then Maria opened the box and moved aside the tissue, sighing with the same sort of delight Rita had exhibited herself upon seeing what was inside.

"Oh, it's beautiful," she said as she carefully withdrew the crystal heart from inside the box.

"Yeah, but does it refer to my job, or the guy's feelings for me?" Rita asked.

"And it's also Waterford," Maria added, not answering the question, as she held the heart up to the light. "Which means, A, this guy's got good taste, and B, this guy's got good money."

"How can you tell it's Waterford?" Rita asked, moving to the sofa to sit beside her sister.

"The little seahorse etched on the side," Maria said, pointing to the logo in question. "See?"

Rita did see the logo. What she didn't see was why the purchaser had spent so much money this time. She'd seen the bandaged heart pin in the hospital gift shop for ten dollars, and even with her unpracticed eye, she knew the charm bracelet couldn't have cost much more than that. This, though, was clearly a costly little trinket. Why the sudden leap in price tag?

"Okay, so the first gift came on Valentine's Day," Maria was saying as she admired the crystal heart, "and the second—" She gasped suddenly. "Oh, wow. I just now made the connection. Valentine's Day. The family curse. No wonder you're concerned."

Rita expelled an errant breath and told herself her sister was being silly. Oh, sure, there were plenty of Barones who believed in the curse Lucia Conti had put on the family two generations ago, but Rita had never been one of them. She was too sensible to believe in curses. Well, pretty much. But she'd heard the story like everyone else in the family, and she could see why some of the Barones believed in it.

When Marco Barone, Rita's grandfather and the founder of Baronessa Gelati, had first come to the United States from Sicily in the thirties, he worked as a waiter at Conti's, a restaurant on Prince Street that was owned by friends of his parents, another Sicilian couple. The Contis had a daughter named Lucia, who, it was said, loved Marco very much, and it was always understood between the two families that Lucia and Marco would someday marry. But Marco met and fell in love with Angelica Salvo, who also worked at Conti's, and they married instead. On their wedding day—Valentine's Day—Lucia, it was also said, had put a curse on them and every future generation of Barones. "You got married on Valentine's Day," Lucia was reported to have said, "and may your anniversary day be cursed. A miserable Valentine's Day to both of you, from this day forward."

Of course, not every Valentine's Day had resulted in

misfortune for the Barones. But a number of tragedies, and a lot of things that had gone wrong for the family had happened on that date. On that first Valentine's Day after their wedding, Angelica miscarried her and Marco's first child. Some years later on Valentine's Day, another child of theirs, one of a pair of twin sons, was kidnapped from the hospital nursery when he was only two days old and was never seen again.

And more recently, there had been a professional debacle this past Valentine's Day, when Baronessa Gelati had thrown a huge gala to launch a new flavor, passionfruit. Someone had spiked the gelato prior to the event with habanero peppers, and everyone who tasted it suffered from a burning mouth. One man had even suffered from an attack of anaphylaxis, a serious allergic reaction. It had been a public-relations nightmare that not even PR whiz Gina had been able to handle. The Barones had been forced to hire an outside spin doctor to help get the company's image back on track. They were still seeing repercussions from the incident.

Not the least of which was Gina's marriage to said spin doctor, Flint Kingman, which, now that Rita thought about it, sort of negated the Valentine's Day curse.

But Rita could still see why Maria might bring up the Valentine's Day curse now, even if Rita didn't believe in it herself.

"So the first gift came on Valentine's Day," Maria began again. "And the second gift came on your birthday. Both special occasions," she noted. "But today isn't a—"

"Today is the third anniversary of my first day working at Boston General," Rita said morosely. "Another special occasion of sorts. Whoever's doing this even remembers the day I started working there."

"But that narrows it down," Maria said triumphantly.

"That means whoever's leaving these is definitely someone you work with, and he must have been there three years ago when you started."

Rita rolled her eyes. "Oh, fine. That narrows it down, all right. To about a couple hundred people."

"But it must be someone you work fairly closely with," Maria said. "It's probably someone in CCU."

"But I started in the E.R.," Rita reminded her sister. "And then I worked briefly in geriatrics before I moved to CCU."

"It still must be someone at work," Maria said. "That's where the gifts arrive, and with this anniversary thing, you know that must be it."

It still didn't help, Rita thought. There were scores of people who could be possibilities.

"I think it's kind of sweet, really," Maria said. "Kind of romantic."

"Romantic?" Rita echoed, thinking that was a strange word to be uttered by a Boston University MBA who spent most of her time working. "Since when did you become such a romantic?"

Maria blushed a little at the question, something else Rita thought odd. "I'm not a romantic," she said. But there was something in her tone that suggested otherwise. "I just don't think it's a stalker, that's all. I think it's someone who has a crush on you."

Rita frowned. "Maria, grown men don't have crushes."

"Sure they do," she objected. "And sometimes it's the big, strong, tough guys who are the most susceptible."

Oh, spoken like an idealistic, virginal twenty-three-year-old, Rita thought wryly. Not that Rita should throw stones, seeing as how she was a somewhat idealistic, though definitely virginal twenty-five-year-old. Still, she had seen more of the world than her younger sister had, mostly thanks to that time in the E.R. And she hadn't seen any big, strong, tough guys who would qualify for secret admirer status. Stalker status, surely, but—

Oh, dammit. She'd let that word out again. Somehow, though, deep down, she wasn't any more convinced of that possibility than Maria was. Her instincts were good, and although she couldn't rule out the sinister entirely, Rita still felt more strongly that whoever was leaving the gifts had no intention of hurting her.

But she couldn't be sure.

Of course, she'd been known to be wrong before.

"I don't know what to do," Rita said. "Whether this person is a crazy psycho or not, I don't like getting anonymous gifts. But I don't know how to out the person, either."

Maria nestled the crystal heart back into its tissue bed and replaced the top on the box. "I don't think it's anything to worry about," she said. "But if it makes you feel that uncomfortable, then maybe you should stop wearing the pin and the bracelet. Maybe if you did, your secret admirer would notice, and then maybe he'd say something about it and reveal his identity."

"I suppose it's worth a shot," Rita said absently.

"And if you want to find a new home for this heart..." her sister added with a smile, holding up the box meaningfully.

Rita smiled back as she retrieved the box from Maria's grasp. She wasn't sure why she wanted to keep it, but she did. She wasn't sure why she wore the pin and heart to work everyday, either. Maybe, deep down, she did know whoever was leaving the gifts was doing it because he admired her secretly.

And maybe, deep down, something about that made Rita feel nice. She'd never had anyone admire her before. Not

for herself, anyway. She'd had the occasional date in high
school and college, of course, but she'd always wondered
if the guys in question had only asked her out because she
was one of the wealthy Barones. Especially after her
twenty-first birthday, when, like all her siblings, she'd come
into a trust fund worth a million dollars.

Rita had yet to touch her own million, however, and had
instead left it invested, thinking someday she'd need it for
something. She didn't know what. She did know, however,
that she wasn't suited to the social butterfly life, and she
loved working as a nurse. Maybe someday, she thought,
she'd have children, and she could use the money for them.
But her secret admirer obviously didn't know or care about
her wealth, otherwise, he would have revealed himself to
her right off the bat, and would have tried to insinuate
himself into her life. So maybe it was Rita herself, and not
her money, that attracted him. In that respect, she couldn't
help but like him.

"No, the heart is fine where it is," she said as she took
the box from her sister and cradled it in her hand.

She just wished she could say the same for herself. Because in spite of Rita's instincts saying the contrary, Maria
was right in that stalkers tended to target women at their
homes, eventually. Rita wondered if her mystery man knew
where she lived. If it was indeed someone she worked with,
he'd certainly have no trouble locating her. Even if it
wasn't a co-worker, if he'd found her at the hospital, all he
would have to do was follow her home one day to find out
where she lived. Of course, if he'd done that, he'd also
know she walked home alone. And he'd probably know
Gina had moved out. And he'd probably know Maria was
often not at home these days, something Rita was going to
have to ask her younger sister about soon. Which meant he

also probably knew that left Rita home alone much of
the time.

She exhaled a slow, unsteady breath and told herself she
was overreacting. Maria was probably right, too, in that
whoever was doing this was harmless. Rita reminded herself that her instincts were good, and that her instincts told
her she probably had nothing to fear. But in reminding
herself of that, she inescapably reminded herself of something else, too.

That she'd been known to be wrong before.

"Do you have a date for the party next weekend?" Maria asked as she rose to leave. "You did remember the party
next weekend, didn't you, Rita?" she added, probably because she thought Rita didn't remember.

And she was right. Rita didn't. Until now.

"The one at the Baronessa business headquarters?" Maria went on. "The one to launch the family's new PR contest to counter all the bad press from the passionfruit di-
saster? The contest that was Gina's brilliant brainchild? The
contest where the winner gets to name a new flavor of
gelato? Remember that?"

"Oh, no," Rita groaned. "I forgot all about it. There's
been so much going on at work lately."

Her sister frowned at her. "Rita," she said in the scold-
ing tone of voice impatient mothers used with recalcitrant
toddlers. "You *are* going, aren't you? All the Barones are
expected to be there, to show our support for the family
and the business. You have to go. You know you'll never
hear the end of it if you don't."

"Yes, yes, I'm going," Rita assured her sister.

"And you *do* have a date for the party, don't you?"
Maria asked further. "Because you know you'll never hear
the end of it if you don't," she repeated with a smile.

Rita closed her eyes and bit back another groan. What

Maria said was certainly true. The older generation of Barones was crazy for grandchildren and grand-nieces and grand-nephews, and they weren't afraid to let anyone—especially the potential bearers of said grandchildren and grand-nieces and grand-nephews—know it. Whenever a Barone of marriageable age showed up at a family gathering without a date, they were set upon by the older generation, wanting to know how they expected to get married and have children if they remained alone.

With Rita, though, who never brought dates to such events, it was becoming a problem of epic proportions. Naturally, it wouldn't have been a problem had she entered the Sisters of Charity as her sister Colleen had. Religious conviction was the only acceptable excuse for such longstanding abstinence from a social life. And even trying to use Colleen as an excuse these days didn't wash, seeing as how she had left the Sisters of Charity not long ago and was now engaged to her college love.

"Um, actually..." Rita began. But she couldn't quite make herself finish the revelation.

"Rita," Maria said again in that same motherish tone, "you haven't even invited a date yet?"

"I forgot, all right?" Rita said.

"And you probably don't have anything to wear, either, do you?"

"Well..."

"Fine," Maria said in a voice of put-upon patience. "I'll take off early Monday and we can go shopping. I wouldn't mind picking up something new myself. The date, though..." she added, letting her voice trail off meaningfully.

"I know," Rita said. "I'll take care of it. I promise."

Though how she was going to keep that promise was beyond her. This event was going to be a stellar, five-star, formal event. It called for someone suave, someone debonair, someone who was tall, dark and handsome, and sophisticated, distinguished and well-connected. Someone like…

For some reason, an image of Dr. Matthew Grayson popped into Rita's head just then. And just as quickly, she shoved the image right back out again. No way was she going to ask Dr. Grayson to this thing. Not only would the two of them have nothing to talk about and feel awkward around each other all evening, but the last thing she needed was for her aunt Sandra to start asking him when he was going to make an honest woman out of Rita.

Uh-uh. No way.

"I'll find someone," she promised her sister again. She just hoped it was a promise she could keep.

Three

Matthew knew plenty of physicians who preferred to get in their rounds early in the day—some of them before the sun even came up—but he wasn't one of them. He'd never been a morning person by nature, and contrary to the desires of some doctors, he liked to see his patients when their family members might be visiting, to answer any questions or alleviate any concerns they might have. So he rarely began his own rounds before ten in the morning, which often meant he ate lunch late.

Monday was no exception, except that he never ate lunch at all. For some reason, his rounds took longer than usual—possibly because Mrs. Harold Asgaard had roughly a million more questions and concerns than the average patient's family members did—so it was after three o'clock before Matthew had a chance for lunch. By then it was so late, he decided he might as well hold off a bit longer and have an early dinner.

Until he went to the hospital cafeteria for a cup of coffee to tide him over and saw Rita Barone seated all alone at one of the far tables.

She wasn't eating, and was instead wrapped up in reading a fat paperback. She was still dressed in her blue scrubs, and still had her hair woven into one of those elaborate braids she favored for work. There were other times, Matthew recalled, when she wore her hair twisted up at the back of her head in a style that reminded him of Grace Kelly—though Rita Barone was much more exciting and exotic-looking than the pale, fragile Grace. Invariably, at work, she had her hair tightly bound in one way or another.

It occurred to him then, not for the first time, that he'd never seen her wear her hair loose. He'd never even seen her in street clothes. Because he'd never seen her anywhere other than work. He knew her hair must be long, because her braid fell past the base of her neck, and he knew it must be thick, because a wealth of the dark tresses fell over her forehead. But he didn't know if it was straight or wavy or curly. And for some reason, suddenly, he wanted very badly to know which it was.

But that wasn't the reason why he strode over to her table after buying his cup of coffee. No, the reason for that was...

Ah, hell. He didn't have a reason for that, he realized as he came to a stop beside her. Which posed a problem for him when she glanced up to see him standing there.

"Dr. Grayson," she said when she saw him, an unmistakable note of surprise lacing her voice.

"Rita," he replied in his usual terse way, wishing he knew of some other way to be besides terse. It made him uncomfortable that all the nurses 'addressed him as "Dr. Grayson" when he addressed all of them by their first names. But it made him even more uncomfortable to extend an invitation to them to address him less formally. He just wasn't sure how to go about being informal, as much as he might like to try it on occasion.

Like this occasion, for instance.

She waited for him to say something more but, God help him, his mind went completely blank. All he could do was gaze into her dark, soulful eyes and try to lose himself completely in their bewitching depths. Rita continued to gaze at him expectantly, however, so when he was finally able to grasp some semblance of coherent thought again, he said the first thing that finally popped into his head.

"Is this seat taken?"

Immediately after uttering it, Matthew cursed himself inwardly. He had revealed way too much about himself in that one short question. That he was an idiot, because he'd just asked a question for which there was an obvious answer. That he was trite, because the question was such a cliché. And, worst of all, that he might potentially be hitting on Rita with that clichéd, idiotic question, because why else would a man ask to sit with a woman unless he was interested in her?

She arrowed her dark eyebrows down in confusion, then glanced over at the obviously empty chair he indicated, then around at the obviously empty cafeteria surrounding them before she finally returned her attention to him.

"Ah, no," she said. "No, it's not taken. Help yourself."

To walk away now would *really* make him look like an idiot. Not that he wanted to turn down her invitation, anyway. He just wished he was a more socially adept person. And he wished he could spend more than a few seconds in Rita Barone's presence without feeling as nervous as a teenager.

"Thank you," he managed to mutter, and with a surprising amount of dignity he seated himself across from her. But for the life of him, he could think of nothing else to say.

Rita closed her book, then looked at Matthew expectantly again.

"I, ah, I hate to eat alone," he said by way of an explanation for his inexplicable behavior.

Rita smiled at him, and something inside Matthew went *zing*. Honestly. *Zing*. How unmanly. If strangely pleasant.

"You're not eating," she pointed out, and suddenly the zinging stopped, only to be replaced by what felt like crashing and burning.

"I hate to drink alone, too," he quickly countered. Oh, score one for the surgeon, he thought wryly. Quite the quipper he was today.

Rita eyed him thoughtfully for a moment, as if she were trying to decide whether she should say what she was thinking. "Interesting you should say that," she finally said. "Because I rarely see you drinking or eating any way *but* alone."

Matthew was too busy digesting the implication of her statement to be bothered by the statement itself. Obviously she'd noticed that he generally spent his time alone. She'd noticed *him*. He couldn't imagine why a woman like her would pay attention to a man like him.

"Just because I drink and eat alone," he said, "doesn't mean I like it." He was surprised by both having spoken the words and by the discovery that they were true.

Rita dipped her chin forward in acknowledgment. "Then by all means, stay as long as you like. I'll be glad to keep you company."

That surprised him, too. But before he had a chance to ponder her statement further, she continued.

"I'm off the clock," she told him, "but I'm waiting for

my sister Maria. She's supposed to meet me here at three-thirty to take me shopping.''

She uttered the last word as if it were the cruelest punishment inflicted in the deepest circle of hell. Matthew couldn't help but smile in response. ''Don't like shopping?'' he asked.

She made a face. ''Well, let's just say there are other things I'd enjoy more. A lengthy discourse on the mating rituals of the common earthworm, perhaps. Or an in-depth introspective on the Monroe Doctrine. Or watching cheese age. That kind of thing.''

He chuckled in spite of himself, and was again surprised by how good it felt to do that. He really should do it more often, he thought. Problem was, he didn't often have the opportunity. ''I thought a love for shopping was encoded into that second X chromosome you women have,'' he said lightly.

''Ah, ah, ah, Dr. Grayson,'' she chided playfully, ''that narrow-minded assumption about women encoded into your Y chromosome is showing.''

''Touché,'' he said, grinning. And then he realized how strange it felt to be doing that, too, because he so rarely did.

What was even stranger was that Rita grinned back. Women hardly ever smiled at Matthew. Probably, he thought, because he rarely gave them a reason to. But Rita Barone was a woman he would like to have smiling at him more often. And not just because she had such a beautiful smile, either. But because of the astonishingly good way it made him feel to see it.

''Maria, though, is not only a good shopper,'' Rita continued conversationally, ''she has good fashion sense, which I utterly lack.''

''And you'd be needing fashion sense because…?''

She made another face, this one even more eloquent than the first. "I have a family thing," she said.

Funny, Matthew thought, his grin failing, but she sounded like she enjoyed family gatherings about as much as he did.

"Not into family values?" he asked, hoping his voice betrayed none of the sourness he felt.

"No, it's not that," she hastened to clarify. "I mean, I love getting together with my family. They're wonderful. It's just…"

"What?"

She sighed fitfully. "Well, the Barones are a *big* family," she began.

Which, of course, was something Matthew already knew. In fact, everyone in Boston knew that. The Barones were well-known even beyond Boston as the founders of Baronessa Gelati, an Italian ice-cream business they'd built up from a single ice-cream parlor in the North End to a chain of popular stores across the country. Baronessa Gelati was also available in all major grocery stores in dozens of flavors. Matthew's favorite, for instance, was double chocolate mocha raspberry mint.

They were well-known for other things, too, Matthew knew. Like their long-standing feud with the Conti family, another renowned Boston family. Matthew wasn't entirely sure what the source of the feud was, but he, like everyone else in the city, was aware of bad blood between the two families over something that had happened decades ago.

"…and anyway, I need a dress for it," Rita was saying, and only then did he realize that his mind had been wandering—probably because he'd been gazing so deeply into her soulful brown eyes—and he'd heard scarcely a word of what she'd said.

"I'm sorry," he said, "but what kind of function did you say it was?"

Rita smiled again. And again went the zinging of his insides. And somehow, it didn't feel quite so unmanly this time. On the contrary, this time, when Matthew noted Rita's smile, he felt very manly indeed.

"I guess I didn't say, did I?" Rita said. "I was so busy going off on trying to avoid all the family prying that goes on at any gathering of the Barone clan."

"Prying?" Matthew asked.

"You know, all the questions the older generation asks about when I'm going to get married and start a family because my biological clock is ticking and I won't be young forever, and there are so many handsome young doctors at Boston General, why haven't I caught one yet?"

Despite the fact that he himself wasn't one of those handsome, young doctors, Matthew stopped himself from asking Rita that very question himself, even if he wanted to know the answer to it. He did sometimes wonder why she wasn't married. A woman like her should at least be involved in a long-term relationship. But he knew she didn't have a boyfriend.

So instead, he found himself commiserating with her. "I have the same problem with my family," he told her. "Only I imagine it's even worse, since I've held out much longer than you have."

"Hey, I bet I can hold out as long as you," she said, smiling even more broadly.

Somehow, though, Matthew couldn't bring himself to smile back. Probably because her assertion didn't make him feel particularly happy for some reason. "I just meant that my family wouldn't mind marrying me off, too," he said.

What he didn't add was, provided it was to the right sort of woman. Well, what the Graysons considered right, at any rate, which meant old-moneyed, blue-blooded, upper-crusted, fair-haired and fine-boned. Someone at the completely opposite end of the spectrum from Rita Barone.

"I guess it's one of those things you just have to put up with once you get out of college," he added, nudging thoughts about his family from his brain, since there were other, infinitely more enjoyable things to think about. Like, say, Rita Barone. "The nosy questions from relatives, I mean."

Just as it occurred to Matthew that he'd spent several minutes making perfectly harmless, wholly comfortable conversation with another person—something he couldn't recall ever doing—he saw Rita glance over his shoulder and lift a hand in greeting to someone. When he turned around, he saw a young woman who looked very much like Rita striding toward them. Her sister, he presumed. Which meant Rita would be leaving now, and he'd be left on his own, alone again.

Normally, it would have made Matthew feel better, since solitude was what he craved most in his life. Suddenly, though, for some reason, he didn't want to be alone. Not unless Rita Barone was alone with him.

Rita's sister—Maria, he recalled her name now—was the epitome of the professional businesswoman, dressed in a smart gray suit and low-heeled pumps. She stopped at the side of the table, leveling first a curious gaze on Matthew, and then a meaningful one on Rita.

With what sounded like a much-put-upon sigh, Rita introduced the two of them. "Maria Barone, Dr. Matthew Grayson. Dr. Grayson, my sister Maria."

"Nice to meet you," Maria said cordially. Then, to her sister, she added pointedly, "Why don't you ask him?"

Rita's eyes widened in clear horror at the suggestion.

Whatever it was, Matthew thought, since he had no idea what Maria was talking about.

Rita, however, evidently did, because she colored furiously and hissed, "Maria!" with a note of unmistakable warning.

The second Barone, though, clearly unfazed by her sister's outburst, turned to Matthew. "Rita needs a date for a big shindig we Barones are putting together this weekend. Otherwise, the rest of the family is going to badger her mercilessly about coming alone. She always comes stag to these things, and I think the older generation is beginning to wonder if she'll ever have a date with anyone."

In response to this, Matthew noticed that Rita blushed even more furiously—at least, he noticed that before she covered her face with her hands. Then she hissed an even more vicious, "Maria!"

"Personally, I don't see anything wrong with a woman going stag to a party," Maria continued blithely, clearly oblivious to—or else totally unconcerned about—her sister's reaction. "But we Barones are very traditional. We're big on old-country values. Especially marriage. And children. Which, of course, is obvious, since Rita and I have six brothers and sisters, not to mention four cousins."

Instead of hissing her response this time, Matthew noticed Rita only groaned.

"Not that I expect you two to get married and have eight kids," Maria continued, "but since you are sitting here talking, I figure you must be friends, so why shouldn't Rita ask you to be her date, you know?"

Logically, it made sense, Matthew thought. Sort of. Socially, it was totally acceptable. In just about every other way, however, it was completely undoable. Because... because...

Well, just because, that was why. And it was a good reason, too, dammit.

"So what do you say, Rita?" Maria asked. "Why don't you ask Dr. Grayson to come to the party with you Friday? Provided he's not otherwise engaged, I mean."

This time Rita only shook her head—still buried in her hands—in response to her sister's question.

"Unless, of course," Maria went on, "you've asked someone else." She began to laugh, as if she'd just made a little joke. "I was being sarcastic," she told Matthew. "Rita never dates anyone."

Another grim sound came from Rita's general direction.

"So, Rita," Maria tried again, "what do you say?"

Finally, Rita dropped her hands from in front of her face and turned to look at Matthew full-on. She was still blushing, but she roused a halfway decent smile. "I hope you enjoyed getting to know my sister," she said. "You'll be reading about her in tomorrow's paper. In the obituaries," she clarified enthusiastically. "Just ignore her," she added before he had a chance to comment. "She didn't mean it."

"Of course I meant it," Maria said.

"I'd love to go with you," Matthew said at the same time.

And he was as astonished to realize he had said it as Rita obviously was to have heard it.

Maria, however, seemed completely unsurprised. "See there?" she told her sister. "I got you a date. Now I can get you an outfit. You can thank me for both later. You ready to go?"

But Rita clearly wasn't listening to her sister, Matthew realized. No, she was much too focused on him.

"Are you serious?" she asked. "You'd really go with me?"

Matthew was surprised by her response. What man

would turn down the invitation to accompany Rita Barone to the ends of the earth on bare feet, never mind to a high-profile, high-society party?

But truth be told, he was surprised, too, by his easy acceptance. Usually he didn't do parties, especially with people he didn't know. In fact, he avoided large groups of people whenever he could, never having felt comfortable among them as an adult because he'd never been welcomed into them as a youth. The scars on his face might be less horrific now than they had been when he was young, but there had been a time in his life—a critical time, and a time that didn't feel so far in his past, even though decades had gone by—when he'd been disfigured in a way that had made people instinctively turn away from him, and then deliberately exclude him. And those vivid memories had stayed with him too well.

Somehow, though, he couldn't bring himself to say no to Rita—or, rather, her sister.

"Of course I'm serious," he made himself say before he could chicken out. "It sounds like fun. After all, the Barones are something of a celebrity clan in Boston. There would be a certain air of distinction in attending."

That was true. The event would be high-profile, high-visibility and high-society. As much as his own family might object to the nouveau-riche, scandal-ridden Barones, the Graysons still traveled in the same social circles, and, financially, at any rate, they were equals. So maybe in attending this bash with Rita, Matthew could bridge some small gap between the two families.

He tried not to think about why that might be important.

"What time should I pick you up?" he asked when Rita only sat there staring at him incredulously.

Or maybe she was staring at him distractedly, he thought. No, that was only thinking wishfully. Maybe she was panicked at the thought of spending time with him and was scrambling for an excuse to get out of going with him. After all, it had been her sister who had made the suggestion. Technically, Rita hadn't invited him at all. So maybe she was just trying to think of a way to let him down gently.

Then she smiled. And only then did Matthew realize he had been holding his breath. He released it in a long, slow expulsion of relief.

"No, I'll pick you up," she told him, smiling a smile of genuine delight. "For an event this big, they always send a car for the family members. It'll swing by for me first, then we'll come by your place. At, say…seven?" she asked.

Matthew nodded. "Seven it is."

She smiled again, and he told himself not to get his hopes up. Strangely, though, he didn't listen to himself at all.

"Great," she said. "Friday at seven. Be there, or be square." With that, she rose from her chair and began to follow her sister out of the cafeteria.

He watched her go, mostly because he couldn't resist doing so, and as she reached the exit, she turned once more to look at him. She smiled one final time and lifted her hand in a quick wave.

Only then did he notice that her wrist was bare, and that she hadn't been wearing the pin either. The pin and bracelet from her secret admirer. Her secret admirer, Dr. Matthew Grayson.

He couldn't help wondering what that meant.

Four

For the rest of that week, Rita felt as if she were walking on eggshells—no, ice-cream cones, a much more appropriate Barone comparison. Whenever she saw Dr. Grayson, she tried to pretend there was nothing different about them just because he was going to be her date—or, rather, escort, she quickly corrected herself.

Except that, somehow, everything felt different.

Suddenly every time she saw him, a funny little burst of heat exploded in her belly, and her mind went blank. She never knew what to say to him after that first hello, so she'd manufacture some excuse to flee his presence before he began thinking her a complete dolt.

She also started noticing things about him that she hadn't noticed before. Like how he put more sugar into his coffee than any health professional should. Like how long and elegant his fingers were—which was hardly surprising for a surgeon. But she was never thinking about him performing surgery when she noticed his hands. Instead she thought about those hands doing other things, things to *her,* things she really shouldn't be thinking about in polite and mixed company. She noticed, too, how broad his shoulders were beneath his white coat. And how he smelled so clean and earthy and masculine. And how his dreamy green eyes seemed to have flecks of blue in them whenever the light hit them just so.

Things like that.

So, by the time Friday evening arrived, Rita just wasn't sure how she was supposed to act. Not around her family when she showed up at Baronessa's executive headquarters with Dr. Grayson at her side, and certainly not around Dr. Grayson himself. As she stood before the mirror in her bedroom at half past six, pondering her reflection, she realized the outfit she had allowed her sister to choose for her was nothing like the kind of outfit she would have chosen for herself.

Talk about your little black dresses…

This particular black dress was just about the littlest one she'd ever seen. And somehow it seemed a lot littler now than it had in the dressing room of Lord & Taylor. In spite of her efforts, the hemline kept creeping several inches above her knees, the neckline kept creeping several inches below her neck, and the cap sleeves several inches away from her collarbones. Granted, Maria had said the dress was supposed to be "off the shoulder," but Rita couldn't help thinking this dress was going to be off way more than her shoulders before the night was through.

Then, when she realized how that thought had come out, she really began to panic. She told herself there was no way her dress would be going off anywhere tonight. Dr. Grayson was much too professional a man ever to try anything like that with a co-worker. And Rita had promised herself a long time ago that when she gave herself to a man it would be because she was utterly and irrevocably in love with him. And she wasn't in love with Dr. Grayson. Not utterly, not irrevocably, not any way. Ergo, the only place her dress was going tonight was back in her own closet.

Besides, she thought further as she tried to tug down the hem again, the garment was so tight, it was bound to cling to her body like a second skin. Somehow, though, that realization wasn't particularly reassuring, either.

She had accessorized the dress with a pearl choker, bracelet and earrings that had belonged to her Nonna Barone. And then she had slipped on the smoky black stockings Maria had also made her buy during their shop-till-they-drop excursion—real stockings, too, the kind you had to wear with a garter belt, even though Rita had protested that such an ensemble was archaic and uncomfortable, and more than a little silly.

But Maria had laughed off her objections, had insisted that wearing such a garment would make Rita feel feminine and playful and even a little powerful—Maria had read all about it in *Cosmopolitan,* after all—and that feeling that way would help Rita battle the nervousness she felt around Matthew Grayson. When Rita had asked her sister what made her think she felt nervous around Matthew Grayson, Maria had only smiled a secret little smile and had pitched the garter belt and stockings—along with a matching black-lace, strapless demi-cup bra—onto the pile of Rita's other purchases.

Now, as nervous as she was—and as reluctant as she was to admit it—Rita did feel more feminine and playful than she normally did. And, oddly, she felt a little more powerful. Maria had told her that she shouldn't want to be practical tonight, not when she was taking ''that yummy Dr. Grayson'' to the party.

That yummy Dr. Grayson, Rita repeated to herself as she pulled a brush one last time through her hair, which she'd opted to wear loose. Funny, but she'd never thought of him as yummy before. Other things, certainly, including intense, intriguing and enigmatic. And, oh, all right, handsome, too, in an imperfect kind of way. And, yes, sexy, as well. She admitted that. But not yummy. That was too frivolous a word for Dr. Matthew Grayson. What he was was…

Delicious.

Rita closed her eyes and made herself turn away from the mirror. He was *not* delicious, she told herself. He wasn't. He was Dr. Matthew Grayson, gruff, distant co-worker. And why had that funny little heat exploded in her belly again all of a sudden, when he wasn't even around to cause it?

With one final, deep breath, she opened her eyes and straightened her shoulders and told herself there was no reason for her to be nervous. She would be surrounded tonight by family and friends she'd known forever, and they would be celebrating a new direction for the family business that was bound to put Baronessa Gelati back on its feet after the debacles and scandals of the last two months. She would be festive and happy and bright.

Even if there was a funny little heat exploding in her belly at every thought she had about Matthew Grayson.

The executive headquarters of Baronessa Gelati were located near the Prudential Center on Huntington Avenue, in a five-story glass-and-chrome building that was ultra-modern, ultra-elegant and ultra-sleek. To Matthew's way of thinking, the structure was reflective of the Barones themselves, fresh and brash and stylish. Rita gave him a brief history and overview of Baronessa Gelati as they took the elevator to the very top of the building, where she said the

offices of the CEO, COO and CFO were located—and also
where the party would be held. Marketing and PR, she told
him as they passed it, were located on the fourth floor,
while the actual manufacturing plant was located just west
of Boston in Brookline. In addition to those two business
locales, she told him, the Barones had a family compound
in Harwichport, on Cape Cod, to which they retreated on
a fairly regular basis for holidays and such.

"Of course, I don't visit as often as some of my brothers
and sisters and cousins do," Rita said as they stepped off
the elevator and into the world of Baronessa Gelati. "What
with work and everything, it's hard to take off for any
length of time. Still, it's a wonderful house and location.
Maybe sometime—"

She halted mid-sentence, without completing the
thought, even though Matthew was fairly sure she had been
about to extend another invitation to him, one that included
joining her and her family there sometime. Or had she
halted because, deep down, she really didn't wanted to pro-
long their liaison, or because she was afraid he would say
no? The possibilities, he thought, were fascinating.

As was Rita Barone.

He still couldn't get over how beautiful she looked. He'd
thought her pretty since the first day he had seen her, but
dressed as she was tonight, *pretty* was far too tame a word
for her. His mental thesaurus could conjure some much
more appropriate ones with fairly little effort. *Gorgeous.*
Stunning. Ravishing. Magnificent.

Those were good for a start.

When he'd opened his front door to find her on the other
side, he had been immediately glad that he'd opted for his
best, most elegant dark suit, white dress shirt and silk tie.
But after that, the only thing he'd been able to register was
all that skin on Rita. And how soft and supple and darkly

exotic it was. He'd never seen her in anything but her scrubs, and he hadn't been able to help himself as he'd skimmed his gaze over her from head to toe and back again, noting the soft swells of her breasts peeking out of the top of her dress, and the long, long legs beneath.

And her hair. Finally, he knew how long it was, shimmering with dark fire as it cascaded to the middle of her shoulder blades. Straight and thick and silky, it was the kind of hair that drew a man's hand, and Matthew had been battling the urge to reach out to her all evening. Not just to touch her hair, either. No, there were lots of places on Rita Barone he'd like to touch. But not here, he quickly amended. Not surrounded by members of her family. It would be much better to touch Rita later, when they were alone.

But he was getting ahead of himself there. Farther ahead than he'd actually ever be, no doubt. Because Rita had offered no sign that this evening was going to be anything other than a family gathering to which she had invited a co-worker, and only because she needed an escort to prevent her from being harassed by family members about her state of singleness. Unless, of course, he took as a sign that dress she was *almost* wearing.

The dress that her *sister* had picked out for her, a little voice in his head reminded him when he recalled their conversation of Monday. So even the dress couldn't be construed as a sign. He'd have to rely on Rita herself for those. And unless he could convince himself that meaningless small talk was a come-on, she'd offered no indication she wanted anything more from him tonight than his simple companionship.

So far.

Speaking of meaningless small talk, he remembered then that they were supposed to be engaged in that activity. So he leapt on her final statement, especially since she had voiced something about which he had always been curious anyway.

"Why didn't you go into the family business?" he asked. "After all, the name Barone is synonymous with Italian ice cream here in Boston. Why did you pursue a career in nursing instead?"

Rita shrugged as she thought about it. "I don't know," she told him. "I got a toy nurse kit for Christmas when I was five, and there was just no going back after that. I can't remember ever wanting to be anything but a nurse. I mean, I could have gone into the business, I guess, if I'd wanted to. But I'm not especially business-minded, and I really never had that much of an interest in it. Not like some of my brothers and sisters did. Nicholas is COO, Joe is CFO, Gina is the VP of marketing and PR, and Maria manages the original Baronessa Gelateria on Hanover Street. But there *are* eight of us," she reminded him. "And cousins, too. My cousins Derrick and Emily both work for the company. I don't think even Dad could have found a place for all of us. Fortunately, some of us did want to follow other courses. My brother Reese is a day trader. Alex joined the navy. Colleen is a social worker now. My cousin Claudia does volunteer work. And my cousin Daniel..." She smiled. "Well, Daniel is sort of a professional thrill-seeker and playboy."

"Nice work if you can get it," Matthew commented wryly.

"Isn't it, though?" Rita agreed with a chuckle. "Come on, Dr. Grayson. I'll stop talking about them, and you can meet them face-to-face. I'm pretty sure just about everyone will be here tonight, except Reese and Alex."

As she took a step away from him, Matthew remained rooted in place. But he reached out to circle her wrist with loose fingers and pull her back toward himself. She faltered at the unexpectedness of his gesture, then overshot her original position as she stumbled backward, coming to a halt when there was scarcely an inch of space to separate their bodies. Instinctively, she opened her hand against his chest to steady herself, and for one split second, Matthew's entire body went rigid under her touch. When his gaze met hers, he could see that she was startled, though whether it was by his action or by his reaction to her action, he couldn't have said. But she never moved her hand, only pressed it even more intimately against him, as if she were afraid she might fall if she didn't. And he never let go of her wrist, as if he were afraid of something, too.

"What's wrong?" she asked softly, breathlessly, and something about the low, throaty timbre of her voice did funny things to Matthew's insides.

"I'm not going anywhere with you, Rita," he said quietly, "until you promise to stop calling me Dr. Grayson and start calling me Matthew."

She hesitated for a moment, her lips parting slightly, her gaze still locked with his. Her eyes were so dark, so deep and so hypnotic, that he felt as if he were nearly drowning in their bittersweet chocolate depths. Her mouth, too, was so succulent and seductive, he wanted nothing more than to dip his head to hers and brush his lips lightly, once, twice, three times, over hers. So focused on the thought was he, in fact, that he actually began to lower his head to hers, until...

"O-okay," she said, "M-Matthew."

Just like that, the spell was broken and Matthew realized the insanity of his thoughts. He pulled his head back and released her wrist, and Rita, seeming nearly as dazed as he, dropped her hand from his chest and back to her side.

At least he had finally heard her speak his name, he

thought, trying to reassure himself. Even if she hadn't been able to say it without tripping over it. Still, he liked the way she said it. He liked it a lot. When she took a step forward this time—though with a bit less determination than she had shown the first time—he followed her.

As she led him down a long corridor past offices and utility rooms and meeting areas, Matthew heard the faint strains of music drawing nearer, music filled with saxophones, clarinets and the soft brush of drums. Cool jazz. Finally, they turned a corner and cleared another, shorter, corridor, and then found themselves in a massive, glass-enclosed banquet room that had clearly been designed for social functions such as this.

Even from the entry, Matthew could look to the other side of the room and see the lights of Boston twinkling against a dusky sky washed with the deep lavenders and golds of impending sunset. Wispy clouds smudged with purple stretched from one side of the panorama to the other, hinting at the darkness that would come soon. Inside, there were twinkling lights, too, tiny white ones in scores of potted trees situated throughout the room, and crisscrossing the ceiling overhead. In the far corner, he saw the source of the jazzy music, a small combo near which a few couples were dancing. Portable bars and tables of elegant-looking appetizers and finger foods were interspersed throughout, and the place was packed with people.

"Boy, your family certainly knows how to throw a party," Matthew said as he followed Rita inside.

"That they do," she agreed enthusiastically. "Oh, look, there are my parents. We can start at the top of the Barone hierarchy and work our way down," she told him. "Once I get the family introductions out of the way, we can enjoy ourselves without the gloom of nosy questions hanging over us."

Matthew eyed her cautiously. "First tell me who's at the bottom of that hierarchy," he said.

She smiled. "Those of us who have the least illustrious and most difficult jobs," she said. "Like me, for instance."

As ending-up places went, Matthew thought, Rita Barone wasn't such a bad deal. In fact, he thought further, she'd be very nice to end up with. In a variety of ways.

Upon meeting Rita's mother, Moira Reardon Barone, Matthew realized that he needn't be so worried about building a bridge between Rita's family and his own. He'd forgotten that the red-haired, green-eyed current matriarch of the clan was the daughter of a former Massachusetts governor. That ought to go over well with his parents—if indeed there was any need for it to go over well with his parents. Which there *wasn't,* he reminded himself, because there was nothing between him and Rita.

Moira Barone, he also discovered, was gracious and friendly and clearly very interested in her daughter's escort tonight, as was evident immediately after Rita made their introductions.

"A surgeon, you say?" she asked with much interest, leveling an approving smile on her daughter. "Well, well, well. We don't have any doctors in the family. Yet."

"Mother," Rita said with clear warning.

"Which is surprising, really," Moira Barone continued, unbothered by her daughter's admonition, "because there are so very many of us. Oh, yes. A doctor could definitely come in handy."

"And this is my father," Rita hastily interjected, "Carlo Barone. Dad, this is Dr. Matthew Grayson, who works with me at Boston General."

The Barone patriarch had dark hair and eyes like his daughter, but his hair was cut with military precision and was graying at the temples. He stood pretty much eye-to-eye with his daughter, but where Rita was trim and curvy, her father was stocky and powerful-looking. Matthew could easily see him as the driving force behind Baronessa Gelati. Even speaking for only a few minutes, the man came across as vigorous and straightforward.

"You seem to get along well with your parents," Matthew remarked as they parted with the elder Barones after Rita had kissed each on the cheek. He always found it interesting to observe the relationships his peers had with their families, having never had a close alliance with his own. He wasn't sure if that was due to nurture or nature, but the Graysons just weren't the type to get too close. Not physically, and certainly not emotionally.

"I think it helps that I was second to last to be born," she said. "With six kids ahead of me, my parents had a lot of practice. But you're right—we do get along well. They're good parents. Dad was always kind of stern when we were growing up, especially with my older brothers, but he was never overbearing. Well, maybe with Reese, for a while anyway. But he seems to have mellowed over the years. And he always doted on us younger girls. I always kind of thought Nicholas and Reese and Joe broke him in for Gina and Maria and me," she added with another one of those dazzling smiles.

After lifting two stems of white wine from a passing waiter, Rita led Matthew toward a bank of windows overlooking the heart of Boston. But she forsook the spectacular view and instead pointed out some of the other Barones as they passed.

"That's my cousin Derrick," she said in a conspiratorial whisper, pointing discreetly at a tall, thin, tuxedo-clad man with dark hair and hawk-like features who was wearing a dour expression. He was standing at a nearby table and seemed to be trying to make an earth-shattering decision between the shrimp puffs and the mini-quiches. "We've always joked that he's the evil twin. My cousin Daniel," she added, pointing to another man who was a bit fairer and more handsome and athletic-looking than the first, "is Derrick's twin. Fraternal, obviously. But then, Daniel's no angel, either," she continued with a laugh. "Still, the two are like night and day. Daniel's always excelled at sports, and just about everything he touches turns to gold. Derrick, well…" She made a little face. "He tries, but he just doesn't have the touch the way Daniel does. He's always been overshadowed by his brother. And I think he knows it."

"They compete a lot, do they?" Matthew asked.

"In some ways," Rita said. But she seemed to be distracted as she said it, and overly focused on watching her cousin. Her distraction lasted only a moment, however, before she turned to Matthew. "How about you?" she asked. "What's your family like?"

Oh, great, she would have to ask something like that, Matthew thought. Where to begin?

"Small and *very* old Bostonian," he said simply, hoping that would be all she needed to know.

He should have known better.

"Oh, listen to you," she said, chuckling. "You talk as if they came over on the *Mayflower*."

"Well, as a matter of fact…"

Her chuckles ceased and she studied him with frank amazement. "Are you serious?"

"'fraid so."

"The Graysons have been here that long?"

He nodded.

"And they were probably rich and blue-blooded when they got here, too, huh?"

He nodded again. "There are rumors that we can trace

our lineage back to minor royalty in the old country, but I've never pursued that."

"Not the princely type, huh?"

"Let's just say I'm better suited to cardiology."

"Wow, that's pretty amazing. I'm only a second-generation American myself. My grandfather came to the United States from Sicily in 1935 and he waited tables until he started up Baronessa. Rags to riches. Peasant to capitalist. Interesting," she added, "that you and I should come from such different backgrounds only to be standing in the very same place now."

"It is," he agreed. "Very interesting."

"So what about brothers and sisters and cousins and parents?" Rita asked. "What are they like?"

He groped for some acceptable adjectives to describe his family, but the only ones that came to mind weren't particularly flattering. Cool. Distant. Proud. Pale. For all their social distinction, the Graysons had nothing on the warm, affectionate, vivacious Barones.

"I have one younger sister," he finally said, forsaking the adjectives for now.

"Ah-hah, firstborn child," she observed.

"You sound as if you think that's significant," Matthew said, eyeing her suspiciously.

She lifted one rather delectable shoulder in a half shrug. "Maybe it is. Maybe it isn't," she replied cryptically. "So what does this sister do? Do the Graysons have a family business, too?"

Matthew shook his head. "Not really, though I am something of a black sheep. My father is a merchant banker, my mother is a CPA, and my sister is a stockbroker. My cousins, uncles and aunts, too, are all financiers."

Rita laughed. "A successful cardiologist is the black sheep? Boy, what a rogue you are."

"I never said we were interesting," Matthew reminded her.

"Oh, I wouldn't say *that*," she murmured as she lifted her wine to her lips for an idle sip.

He was about to ask her what she'd meant by her comment, but Carlo Barone took to the podium vacated by the jazz combo then, citing his need to make an announcement about an upcoming contest for Baronessa Gelati. Then he introduced Gina Barone Kingman, who Matthew recalled was the VP of PR.

Gina didn't much resemble Rita, however, beyond sharing the same olive complexion. Rita's sister was taller, had light-brown hair that was curly instead of straight, and even from a short distance, Matthew could see that her eyes were light in color, and not the mesmerizing espresso of her younger sister's. Like nearly every woman at the party, she was dressed in a black cocktail dress, though hers covered more of her than Rita's did, as befitted one of the company's executives.

Gina spoke for a few minutes about the history of Baronessa, made a brief mention of having abandoned a recently tested passionfruit flavor, then held up a letter-sized sheet of paper for everyone to see.

"What I have in my hand," she said, "is a list of the rules and requirements for our new Name That Flavor contest. Tomorrow's newspaper will carry this in a full-page ad. We're challenging anyone in the Boston metro area who's inventive and culinarily inclined to develop a recipe for a new gelato flavor."

A smattering of enthusiastic applause went up at this, along with the nodding of several heads.

"All recipes entered," Gina continued as the clapping eased, "will be duplicated and produced in a small batch at the Baronessa factory in Brookline, and a panel of judges that includes the executives of Baronessa and the board of directors—and also Mom," she added with a smile, again to much applause, "—will taste each entry and, among them, choose a winner."

More applause met the announcement.

"The creator of the winning recipe," Gina went on, "will not only see his or her flavor become a reality in Baronessa stores across the country—not to mention supermarkets everywhere—but will also win $1,000 for his or her efforts, which is some pretty nice pocket change."

Amid more applause, Matthew leaned over toward Rita and murmured, "Have they totally abandoned the passion-fruit flavor, then? That sounds like it would be pretty good."

Rita turned to look at him as if she couldn't believe he'd asked her such a thing. "I think that's a safe bet, after the debacle at the launch."

"Have you discovered how the habanero peppers got into the gelato?" Matthew asked.

Rita shook her head. "We have no idea. The family's pretty well divided into two camps. Some think it's someone from a rival ice-cream company, and some think it's the work of the Contis. Do you know about that?" she asked. "The big family feud?"

"I've heard about it," Matthew told her. "I think anyone who's lived in Boston any length of time has."

She nodded. "I don't know, though. I can't see the Contis doing something like that. Personally, I lean toward the corporate sabotage angle. Though even that's hard to believe. I just can't imagine some legitimate business doing something like that."

"You'd be surprised what people are capable of," Matthew said.

And when he said it, his voice carried an edge that Rita

hadn't heard before. Something told her not to pursue it, though, so she changed the topic of conversation to something more innocuous, telling him she hoped that whoever won the contest came up with some variation on chocolate, since that was her own personal favorite.

Gina said a few more words about the contest, outlining the requirements and such, and then the excitement gradually began to settle. After a few more announcements, she encouraged everyone to go back to enjoying the party.

The champagne never stopped flowing for the rest of the night. And since the atmosphere was so festive, and since neither Rita nor Matthew would be responsible for driving home, they both partook freely.

That could be the only reason, Rita decided later, after she had led Matthew out to the terrace adjoining the party room on the top floor of the building to gaze out at the lights of Boston, why she would ask him the question she did once they were finally alone.

"How did you get those scars on your face?" she said before she had even realized she meant to say it.

Immediately, she clapped a hand over her mouth, regretting at once having put voice to the question. But the thought had been circling in her head all night, ever since she'd seen him looking so exquisitely handsome in his expensive suit. She just hadn't been able to stop thinking that if it weren't for those scars, he would be absolutely perfect. And then, suddenly, she was asking how those scars had originated, when she should have kept her mouth shut. Not just because the question had been so frightfully impolite but because Matthew went absolutely rigid when she asked it.

"I'm sorry," she immediately apologized from behind her hand. "I had no right to ask that. Please…forget I said anything."

And then she shivered, though she told herself it was because of the cold April breeze that whirled around the building just then, and not Matthew's glacial stare.

The glacial stare lasted only a moment, though, and then vanished as quickly as it had appeared. He must have noticed her trembling, because his expression softened, and his voice was gentle as he said, "You're cold. I never should have suggested we come out here."

Before she could say anything else, he whipped off his suit jacket and draped it around her shoulders. Rita was going to decline the gesture and suggest they go back inside, but the moment the soft fabric settled over her bare shoulders and arms it began to warm her, and she realized it was Matthew's warmth. And then she noticed that it smelled like Matthew, too, spicy and clean and male, and that having his jacket around her was almost—*almost*—like having his arms around her. Suddenly she didn't want to go back inside. Suddenly she wasn't cold anymore. In fact, heat was starting to seep into parts of her she hadn't even realized were cold until that moment.

"Thank you," she said softly as she pulled the jacket more tightly around herself, reveling in the sensation of having him so close, even if he wasn't standing very near her. Then, once again, she said, "I'm sorry, Matthew. I shouldn't have asked. It's none of my business."

"No, it isn't that," he said quickly. But his voice was still somber and a little distant, as if he were lost in thought. "I just..." He sighed heavily. "It happened so long ago, you'd think it wouldn't be a big deal anymore. That it wouldn't bother me to talk about it."

"But it does?"

"Sometimes."

"Look, honestly, you don't have to tell me if you don't—"

"I was mauled by a lion."

Rita stopped speaking the moment he started, but never quite closed her mouth. She continued to gape at him when he concluded his brief—if shocking—revelation. Frankly, she wasn't sure whether to believe him. Was he joking, trying to make light of what had really happened? Did people actually *get* mauled by lions? It sounded like something from a nineteenth-century novel.

"When I was ten years old," he continued. "My parents and I were on safari in Kenya at the time."

She realized then that he was indeed telling the truth, but she still shook her head in silent disbelief.

"I strayed away from camp one night," he said, his voice quiet, sober, as if he were deep in thought, "even though they'd warned me against doing that. I was looking at the sky," he told her by way of an explanation. Then he turned his head to do that now. He gazed out at the star-spattered darkness above them as if he'd never seen it before. "It was so beautiful that night," he continued, "so clear, and I guess I just didn't realize how far I'd walked. I was like the baby wildebeest who strays from the herd," he added with a halfhearted smile. "Easy prey." His smile fell suddenly and he turned to look at Rita again. "The lion came out of nowhere. A female. One minute everything was quiet and still and magical, and the next..." He met her gaze levelly. "The next minute, I was literally fighting for my life."

"Oh, Matthew," Rita said. She couldn't imagine the confusion and terror he must have felt.

"Someone in the camp must have heard the commotion, because a group came running and screaming and waving torches, and the lion, amazingly, let go of me and disappeared into the darkness. My shoulder and back bore the brunt of the attack," he told her. "You think the scars on my face are something, you should see the ones there." He seemed to realize then that what he'd said might have a double meaning, because he glanced anxiously away and quickly added, "On second thought, no, you shouldn't. The plastic surgeons did what they could with my face, but the first wounds went so deep—"

He didn't finish whatever he'd intended to say. But then, Rita thought, he really didn't have to. She understood. She had no idea what to say to him, however. But when Matthew looked up at her, he seemed so anxious about her response to him that she made herself smile. Then, strangely, she realized that her smile felt like a perfectly natural response.

"I think the plastic surgeons did a wonderful job," she told him. "Of course, they had a good foundation to start with. You could be a movie star."

"I don't know about that," he said, dropping his gaze to the ground again like a bashful teenager. "But the whole thing certainly sounds like something from a movie. I've spent most of my life wishing it were. It wasn't much fun growing up looking like a beast."

He looked thoughtful for a moment, taking great care about whether or not he should say any more. And he gazed up at the sky again when he finally did begin to speak. "I remember once," he said, "when I was in eighth grade. I'd started a new school—again—because I'd gotten thrown out of the last one—again—for fighting so much. Not that I was ever the instigator, mind you," he added parenthetically, as if he needed for her to know that. "But I was in a new school, and like an idiot, I was hoping maybe things would be different this time. And there was a girl in my semantics class—"

His voice drifted off, but had mellowed to the point where Rita knew he was recalling what must have been a pretty powerful crush. She smiled in spite of his somberness.

"She was so pretty," he said with a halfhearted smile. "Blond hair, blue eyes, tight sweaters, every adolescent boy's idea of the perfect girl. And she always turned around whenever I was looking at her, as if she could feel me watching her. But she never seemed to mind, you know? She'd always look at me back. My rational mind told me she looked at me for the same reason everyone looked at me. Because I was a freak—"

"Matthew—" Rita began. But he hurried on before she had a chance to say any more.

"But there was a part of me that wondered, that hoped—" He shrugged. "I don't know. She just seemed to be different from the others. Then, one day, her best friend came up to me at my locker and told me this girl wanted to meet me. That she liked me. That she wanted to talk to me. I couldn't believe it. I was so happy. So I went to meet her behind the gym, where her friend said she'd be waiting for me."

He paused again, inhaling deeply before letting the breath out in a slow, melancholy exhalation. "Long story short," he continued, "the girl was indeed there waiting for me. With her boyfriend. She told me to stop looking at her in class, because I made her sick to her stomach. And then she let her boyfriend do the rest of the talking. Unfortunately, there wasn't much talking after that. And I had to leave that school for another one a few weeks later."

"Oh, Matthew," Rita said again.

"So, there you have it," he concluded flatly. "The life and times of the beast."

Something inside of Rita turned over at that. He couldn't possibly think of himself that way, could he?

"You're not a beast," she said.

He laughed, but there was nothing happy in the sound. "Aren't I?" he asked. "Everyone at the hospital seems to think so."

"That's not because of your scars," Rita was quick to correct him. "It's because of your attitu—" She halted again before finishing, slapping a hand over her mouth again, appalled at what she had just revealed. "Matthew, that's not what I meant," she hastened to clarify, dropping her hand. "You're not a beast," she said again, with more conviction this time.

As if she wanted to prove that, she lifted her hand to his face and, after only a small hesitation, skimmed her fingertips lightly over the scars he seemed to think so repulsive. At first, he jerked his head back, as if he didn't want her to touch him. But she moved her hand forward again, laying her fingers gently over his injured flesh, and this time, for some reason, he let her.

"You're not a beast," she insisted. "You're..."

His eyes met hers again, and she realized that somehow, at some point, they'd moved closer together, and that scarcely a breath of air separated them now. Matthew turned his head just the merest bit, tilting it to the side so that he might enjoy her touch more fully.

"I'm what?" he asked softly, lifting his hand to cover hers.

Now Rita opened her hand completely, pressing her palm gently to his face, cupping his cheek and jaw more completely. She felt herself moving closer still, and didn't recall making the decision to advance. Her instincts seemed to have taken over by then, and all she could do was follow them.

"You're..." she tried again.

But no words came to her aid to describe him. Probably because at that point he was...indescribable. But also very,

very desirable. Something about the way he was looking at her then sent a shudder of emotion spiraling through the center of her. And when he covered her hand with his the way he did, that spiral coiled even tighter.

Not sure why she did it and still following her impulses, Rita pushed herself up on tiptoe and pressed her lips lightly to his. The moment their mouths made contact something inside her ruptured, spilling heat and fire throughout her body. The sensation was so immediate, so intense, so startling that she instinctively pulled away from him again.

A quick peck, she told herself when it was over and she was back on her feet—however precariously. A brief, chaste, perfectly innocuous little kiss. That was all it had been. She had wanted to show him he wasn't repulsive, as he seemed to think. So she had brushed her lips gingerly over his, and then she had pulled away again.

A quick peck, she repeated to herself more firmly. No harm, no foul. Nothing to it. Somehow, though, she felt as if the entire earth had slipped away beneath her feet.

"You're not a beast, Matthew," she said one last time. "Not in any way." And then, because she was afraid of what might happen if they stayed outside—alone—any longer, she stepped back and added, "We should probably go back inside. They'll be looking for us. And it really is colder out here than I thought."

She felt like a big, fat liar as she turned away from him without awaiting a reply and made her way back toward the terrace door. Not just because she knew the last thing the Barones would do was look for her if she'd disappeared with a handsome, distinguished doctor. But because she'd never felt hotter in her life.

Five

What little was left of the evening seemed to drag, as far as Rita was concerned. Well, except for those few occasions when she turned to look at Matthew and caught him studying her with a burning gaze that scorched her from her head to her toes and all points in between. Then again, how could anything so mundane as a glittering high-society party possibly be appealing after that single, perfect kiss she and Matthew had shared out on the terrace?

She could no longer tell herself it had been an innocent little peck to prove a point. Rita knew better. She had kissed Matthew because she had been attracted to him. More than attracted. She had been moved by him. Enchanted by him. And not just this evening, either, but for some time. Only now was she beginning to realize that she had been attracted to him probably since the day she'd begun working in CCU.

Yes, he had been gruff at times, and often standoffish.

But she had always detected something beneath his surface that was almost…vulnerable somehow. Now she knew she had been right to sense such a thing. And now she knew why. He had suffered a horrible experience when he was a child. The physical wounds alone must have been unbearable for him. How must it have felt to grow up looking the way he did, and harbor memories of such a harrowing encounter? It was no wonder he acted the way he did around other people. He'd probably never had the chance to interact with them on a normal, everyday sort of level.

Tonight, hearing him speak the way he had about what had happened to him, she had begun to understand that there was still a wounded little boy inside him who was motivated by fear. And she had wanted to show him that she wasn't scared of him. On the contrary, knowing what had happened to him had only drawn her to him that much more completely. And she'd wanted to show him, too, that he shouldn't be afraid of her.

By mutual and unspoken consent, neither of them mentioned the kiss once they returned to the party. Of course, neither seemed to feel comfortable with the other anymore, either, and neither seemed able to meet the other's gaze— well, except for those few accidental scorching ones Rita had caught from Matthew. And those, she decided, she'd just as soon not mention, either.

She tried to reassure herself that by the time the two of them returned to work Monday morning, the whole thing would be forgotten. They were both bound to spend the weekend convincing themselves that nothing had happened out on the terrace—nothing save a chaste, innocent little peck—and by Monday, surely, they would have succeeded. Because, really, she told herself nothing *had* happened out on the terrace save a chaste, innocent little peck…and an earth-shattering awareness of each other that Rita was certain wouldn't pass anytime soon.

They were doomed.

There was no way either of them would ever feel comfortable around the other at work again. Not that they'd ever felt comfortable around each other at work before, she reminded herself. But she quickly abandoned that train of thought. She was afraid she'd admit how she'd always been attracted to Matthew Grayson—she might even go so far as to say she'd had a crush on him since the day she'd met him. And how *that* was the real reason she'd kissed him tonight.

She knew better than to think her memories of a kiss like that would fizzle out and be forgotten. No, her memories were bound to multiply and intensify until she had no choice but to seek him out and relive the experience. Over and over and over again.

Oh, yeah. They were definitely doomed.

"We should probably go," Rita told him at midnight, when she realized everyone else seemed to be leaving, too. Well, everyone except her family, who would doubtless party until the wee hours. She scanned the room for Maria, but was surprised to see that her sister seemed to have already left. More surprising was the recollection that after badgering Rita so mercilessly about needing a date, Maria hadn't brought anyone to the party tonight.

"I can take a cab home," Matthew offered, obviously still uncomfortable with what had happened out on the terrace and wanting to be free of Rita as soon as was polite.

"No, no, that won't be necessary," she assured him anyway. Mostly, she supposed, because she didn't want him to think there was any reason for them to alter their plans. "The driver is paid for the night," she added, "and he's expecting to take us both home. We might as well take advantage of him.''

The moment that final sentence was out of her mouth, she wished she hadn't said it. It made her want to think about taking advantage of someone else, too.

Matthew seemed to be thinking the same thing, she realized when she braved a glance in his direction, because his cheeks had grown ruddy, and his eyes had darkened dangerously. But he said nothing, only swept his hand toward the exit in a silent indication that Rita should precede him. As she strode past him, he extended his arm to her, crooking his elbow, as if he wanted her to take it. Fearing he might think her a big chicken if she didn't—and also because she yearned to touch him, however superficially—Rita complied, threading her arm through his to walk side-by-side with him to the door.

Although they remained arm-in-arm, they spoke not a word as they descended in the elevator, both of them fixing their gazes on the illuminated, decreasing numbers above the doors. When they exited, they silently crossed the lobby and strode through the big glass front doors, then toward the bank of limos waiting for the various Barones they were to escort home. When they found theirs, the driver hustled out to open the back door for them, and Rita entered with Matthew right behind her. The moment their chauffeur closed the door behind them, however, she tensed.

For the first time since that kiss, she and Matthew were alone. Utterly and completely alone, thanks to a pane of smoked privacy glass that cut off their view of the driver and, Rita knew, the driver's view of them. They were in a much more isolated—and much more intimate—setting now than the public display on the top-floor terrace where anyone might have stumbled upon them at any time. This was a much quieter, much cozier—much darker—environment than the one they had shared before. And it immediately made Rita think about doing things that hadn't occurred to her on the way to the party earlier.

Well, okay, maybe doing those things had occurred to her then, back in some dark, recessed, feverish, sexually deprived part of her brain. Maybe, once or twice, during the drive to the party, she had entertained a quick fantasy of what it would be like to make love with Matthew Grayson on the wide back seat of this very car. He'd just looked so incredibly handsome and sexy in his dark suit, she hadn't been able to help herself. But she'd only thought about it once or twice, only for a few seconds, and certainly not realistically. Now, though, after their kiss, she thought about it for more than a few seconds—and in much more graphic terms.

Oh, good heavens, what was wrong with her? she wondered. This was Matthew Grayson she was fantasizing about. The Beast from Boston General. In spite of all her earlier softening toward him and romanticizing about him, she tried to make herself be realistic. Yes, there were reasons for why he acted the way he did around people. But the fact remained that he *did* act that way. For all she knew, he might not even be capable of falling in love with a woman.

Then again, she chastised herself, what did love have to do with anything? She certainly wasn't in love with him. How had she gotten from hot sex in the back of a limo to hearts and flowers and happily-ever-afters? The two weren't necessarily connected at all.

"Are you going to bring it up, or should I?"

Matthew's deep, resonant voice knifed through the darkness with all the finesse of a finely edged blade, but the question itself hit Rita with the hacking impact of a dull meat cleaver.

"Bring what up?" she asked innocently, hoping that if she pretended she had no idea what he was talking about, Matthew would go along with the ruse.

She should have known better.

"Guess I'll be the one to bring it up then," he said dryly.

"Bring what up?" she tried again. Futilely, she soon learned.

"What happened out on the terrace tonight," he said plainly. "You...kissing me."

Rita started to deny it, started to insist that they had both been the ones involved in that kiss, but she knew she would be lying. Because in spite of his having done nothing to stop it, it had been she who'd kissed him, and she who had ended it. She alone must take responsibility for what had happened. She had kissed Matthew. She only wished she could tell him why.

"I'm not sure what happened," she told him honestly. "I just..." She gave a halfhearted shrug. "It seemed like the thing to do at the time."

He said nothing in response to that, and when she looked at him, his face was cast in shadow, so she had no way to gauge what he might be thinking. Then the limo passed beneath a street lamp, and for one brief second, she caught a glimpse of his face, and she saw that he looked...

Puzzled.

Of all the things she might have expected him to be, puzzled was one that would never have occurred to her. Matthew Grayson had always struck her as someone who would have an answer for every question, an explanation for every mystery. Yet he looked puzzled by what had happened between the two of them earlier that evening.

The realization heartened Rita. It meant they were on equal footing.

Until he said, "So if I kissed *you* this time, what would happen?"

And then, suddenly, things were totally out of whack. A splash of heat spilled through Rita's midsection, not just because of the question itself, but because of the way he uttered it—as if he fully intended to find out.

She swallowed with some difficulty. "Why, um, why would you want to do that?"

Thanks to the darkness, she sensed more than saw him shrug. But even in the darkness, she could tell there was nothing casual in the gesture.

"It just seems like the right thing to do," he told her. She could sense him drawing nearer as he said it.

And then he was kissing her, and she was kissing him back, and a swirl of tempestuous hunger was eddying up inside her. He lifted a hand to the back of her neck and curved his fingers over her nape, his touch warm and insistent and absolute. Her stomach seared with heat at the way his fingers pressed into the tender flesh of her neck, her heart humming with anticipation of what would come next.

Oh, dear heaven, she thought. What was happening? And why couldn't she make it stop? Why didn't she *want* it to stop?

There was none of the tentativeness or uncertainty in Matthew's kiss that had been present in Rita's earlier. No, when Matthew covered her mouth with his, it was with confident determination. He kissed her the way a man must kiss a woman when he knows that he wants her, and when he knows that he can have her. Rita had never been kissed that way before. Not because no man had ever wanted her, but because *she* had never wanted any man enough to allow him to kiss her that way. With Matthew, though...

She wanted. Oh, how she wanted.

Instinctively, she tilted her head to the side a bit, a gesture he used to his advantage to deepen the kiss. The hand at her nape moved to her jaw, and he splayed his fingers wide over her cheek and chin, silently urging her to open her mouth for him. Rita complied willingly, groaning with desire at the surging entrance of his tongue as he tasted her. A wild heat exploded in her belly at the intimate invasion, spreading its fever outward, flooding into her breasts and between her legs. Impulsively, she pressed her hands to his chest, driving one beneath his jacket and up to clutch his shoulder. When she did, Matthew looped his other arm around her waist to pull her closer still.

Her body flush with his now, Rita felt his heat and his hardness permeating his clothing, joining with her own warmth and softness as she touched him. Something inside her went a little wild at the recognition of how their bodies' differences complemented each other so perfectly. She couldn't help wondering in what other ways their bodies could correlate. So she pushed herself against him more urgently, one hand moving now to his hair, her fingers threading through its silky thickness. He seemed to like it when she did that, because a low moan emerged from some dark place deep inside him in response.

The realization that she pleased him made Rita feel bolder, and she tilted her head to the side again. But she used the motion to her own advantage, slipping her tongue into his mouth this time. The sensation of damp heat surrounding her was like nothing she had ever experienced before. Matthew tasted of champagne and caviar, and something dark and masculine and bittersweet. And all Rita could think was that she wanted to experience more of him.

She wasn't sure whether she was responsible for what happened next, or Matthew. But somehow, she ended up sitting in his lap, her legs stretching out across the wide back seat of the limo. She lost a shoe, but she didn't care, and in fact kicked off the other in what she could only think in her agitated state was a wanton effort to free herself from her clothing. Because suddenly, she wanted very much to be free of her clothing. Even more than that, she wanted Matthew to be free of his. Then they would be able to explore each other more completely. And in that heady, feverish moment, as the two of them volleyed for possession of their kiss, Rita realized she wanted very badly to explore as much of Matthew as she could.

He seemed to share her desire, because just as the thought was forming in her brain, she felt his hand glide slowly from her waist, over her hip and along her thigh, to settle at the hem of her dress. As he continued to kiss her, he began to push the fabric higher, inch by subtle inch, over her thighs. Bit by bit, her little black dress grew smaller still, until his fingers cleared the smoky silk of her stockings and met bare flesh. The moment Matthew realized what his fingers had already discovered, he jerked his head back from hers and, panting, gazed down into her face.

"Are you actually wearing what I think you're wearing?" he gasped.

Not trusting herself to speak—or perhaps unable to—Rita could only nod her response.

He studied her in silence for a moment longer, then began stroking the pad of his thumb gently over the bare flesh of her thigh. Every mellow touch set off tiny explosions in its wake, until Rita feared she would spontaneously combust if he didn't stop it. When he skimmed a finger beneath one of the silky garters, she bit back a groan of need.

"It's always been my understanding," he said roughly as he gave the garter a gentle tug, "that women only wear these for a...sexual encounter."

Did they? Rita wondered feverishly. How very interesting. Maybe she should start doing more reading. Who knew what else she might learn? All she was able to manage by way of a response, though, was a breathless, honestly offered, "It's the first time I've worn one."

"Really?" he asked with much interest.

Now she was only able to nod in response.

"I've never known a woman who wore one," he said.

Somehow, that surprised Rita. In spite of his scarred face and distant disposition, he seemed like the kind of man who would be well versed in the ways of women. Then he kissed her again, in a way that let her know he was indeed. And then she ceased thinking at all when he began tasting her deeply once more, and the fingers at her thigh began strumming over her sensitive flesh again. All Rita could do then was cup his face in her hands, turn her head to the side and kiss him back for all she was worth.

As she kissed him, she registered the movement of his hand along her thigh again, pushing the fabric of her dress higher still, until his fingers made contact with the edge of her black lacy panties. He halted there for a moment, as if he weren't sure she would allow him any further liberties, so Rita shoved her fingers into his hair again and deepened their kiss, fairly devouring him this time. He seemed to understand her eagerness, because he pushed up her dress farther, until he could cup his whole hand possessively over the right side of her lace-covered derriere.

That was when he tore his mouth from hers and pressed his face into the juncture of her neck and shoulder, murmuring something incoherent against her hot flesh before nipping it lightly with his teeth. Rita did groan this time, needfully, brazenly, then turned herself on his lap to give him freer access to her. In doing so, she felt him surge to life beneath her, swelling hard and heavy and ready for her.

The hand on her bottom clenched tight at her movement, and she bit back another feral sound. Then she dipped her head to his again, ravaging his mouth this time in a kiss full of demand.

By now he had pushed her dress up around her waist, so Rita turned her entire body to straddle his lap. She was thankful for the smoky, one-way glass between them and their driver and the outside world. Still, the fact that they were cruising through downtown Boston as they lost control only made it that much more exciting for her. Now as she faced Matthew fully, as her eyes met his in the dim light, she realized he looked like a man who was about to come undone. So, to help him along, she leaned forward. Instead of taking his mouth in a hungry kiss this time, she only brushed her lips lightly over his, once, twice, three times. Then, having no idea what possessed her to do it, she pulled back again, reaching behind herself to slowly, so slowly, draw down the zipper on her dress.

At first, he seemed not to realize what she was doing. But when she tugged the dress down over her arms, pushing it down around her waist, he had no choice but to notice. Without a word, his gaze never leaving hers, he lifted both hands and covered each of her black-lace-covered breasts. With one deft move, he bared a breast so that he could fill his hand with her naked flesh. He palmed the soft globe first in slow, gentle circles, his hand warm on her skin, confident, almost courtly.

Rita closed her eyes as he touched her, to better enjoy the sensation. And when she felt his mouth open over the tumid peak, she sighed eloquently and tangled her fingers in his hair. For long moments he sucked at her, pushing her breast higher with his hand, pulling her deep into his mouth, the damp pressure tugging at something too-long buried inside her. He laved her with the flat of his tongue, then teased her with its tip, then sucked harder still. Never in her life had she felt such an extraordinary sensation. And the pleasure winding through her was something she never wanted to have end.

"Take me home with you tonight," she said breathlessly as he traced the lower curve of her breast with his tongue.

She had no idea what made her utter the command, nor, really, what she was asking him to do. She only knew that she couldn't leave him yet, not after the things he had just introduced her to. She only knew that she wanted, needed, to be with him. Needed to know what else he could make her feel.

"Please, Matthew," she said again, her fingers convulsing in his hair as he dragged his open mouth up over her breast again. "Please take me home with you tonight. I want..."

But truly, she wasn't sure what she wanted. She only knew that, in that moment, she could not leave him. Not feeling as unsatisfied as she did.

Matthew drew back at her breathlessly offered request, and when she opened her eyes, she saw that he was gazing at her. But she couldn't discern his reaction.

"Are you sure?" he asked softly.

She nodded eagerly, even though she felt anything but certain. She reminded herself ruthlessly of the promise she had made to herself, that the first time she made love with a man would be because he would be someone special. But then she realized she had never felt more special than she did at that moment. Matthew made her feel special. He was special, too. He was... Well, he was everything. Everything she had always wanted in a man. Handsome, smart, sexy and kind. And he made her feel things... Oh, how he made her feel.

He would be an attentive lover, she thought further, considering the ways he had touched and pleasured her so far. She tried not to think about how much practice he must have had over the years, and focused instead on how he was here with her now. He had been gentle with her so far, and she sensed he would be gentle throughout. And that was what she wanted—and needed—for her first time. Most of all, though, she cared for Matthew, maybe more than she was willing to admit.

Of course, she'd always sworn she would be in love with the man her first time. But she was twenty-five years old, she reflected, and had yet to fall in love. Maybe love, she thought, was asking too much. Maybe for her first time it would be enough to admire and respect and care for her partner.

Matthew, she told herself in that moment, would be perfect.

"If I take you home, Rita," he said, his voice still soft, but now steeled with intent, "there won't be any turning back. Do you understand?"

She nodded again.

He lifted a hand to her face, framing her jaw in his palm before moving his fingers to her hair and brushing it back from her face. "Once we're inside, I'm going to lock the door and spend the entire night making love to you. And once I make love to you…"

He said nothing more after that, only met her gaze levelly in the darkness, with an unmistakable intent. She wasn't sure if he was telling her that after they made love nothing would change between them, or if everything would change. Somehow, though, in that moment, Rita didn't care. She only knew she wanted Matthew. More than she had ever wanted anything in her life. And she knew, too, that she would have him.

"I understand," she said.

Deep down, though, she wasn't sure she understood at all.

Six

Rita saw Matthew nod slowly in response to her assertion that she understood. Then he ran his hand over the crown of her head one final time, leaned forward to give her breast one long, final, leisurely taste, then, with clear reluctance, tugged up her brassiere and helped her back into her dress. For now. Even though she was shaking almost uncontrollably, Rita moved from his lap to the seat beside him just as the limo rolled to a stop in front of his brick townhouse, and she only barely managed to pull her dress down over her thighs and scoot her feet back into her shoes before their driver opened the door on Matthew's side.

He exited the car with grace and style, and no one ever would have suspected that only a moment ago he had been pleasuring a woman with her breast in his mouth. Rita, on the other hand, exited the car with anything but grace and style, because her entire body was trembling with what had just transpired between the two of them, and her mind was scrambled with thoughts about what was to come.

Matthew seemed to understand her state of agitation, because he draped his arm over her shoulder and pulled her close the moment she stood. Rita made minimal small talk with their driver and sent him on his way with assurances from Matthew that he would take her home after the two of them shared a nightcap here. She had no idea if the driver believed them, and frankly, she didn't care. She had far more important things to think about at the moment. Especially when Matthew began to guide her up the walkway toward his house.

He unlocked the front door and pushed it open wide, then stood aside to let Rita enter first. He crossed the threshold immediately behind her, closed the door and locked it, then reached for her and hauled her back against him.

His kiss this time was hot and demanding, with absolutely no pretense of taking things slowly. He moved his hand to the zipper of her dress and pushed it down, down, down, past her waist and over her hips, until he could spread the fabric open wide. He made short work of her bra, as well, and then she felt his hands on her bare back, rushing over her naked flesh as if he wanted to learn every inch of her. As he explored her, Rita went to work on his clothing, jerking loose his tie and tossing it to the floor, then freeing the buttons on his shirt one by frantic one. She shoved it and his jacket off his shoulders together, both garments falling to the floor alongside his tie. Then he pushed her dress down over her hips and thighs, letting it fall to her ankles. Rita stepped out of it and kicked it aside, and then they both stood half-naked and panting in the foyer.

A slash of pale light spilled over them from a lamp he had left burning in the living room beyond, and in that pale light, Rita drank her fill of him. He had a magnificent physique, lean and athletic, his chest corded with solid muscle, his biceps and forearms salient beneath his bronzed skin. She had heard him speak of skiing in winter and tennis in summer, and it showed. She traced both of her index fingers along the lines of his muscular shoulders, down over his biceps, along the solid forearms to the hands he had settled at her waist. Then she traced the route back up again.

At his left shoulder, though, she halted, noting for the first time the pucker of a wide scar that ran to nearly the center of his chest. She recalled then that he had said his shoulder and back had suffered the brunt of his attack, and she closed her entire hand gingerly over the scarred flesh of his shoulder.

"Don't," he said softly, shrugging out from beneath her touch.

But Rita followed his movement, closing her hand over him again. "I want to see, Matthew," she said softly.

But he shook his head. "Women don't react well to the sight," he told her decisively.

She tried not to think about how many women, then told herself it didn't matter. All that mattered was that the two of them were here together now. Everything that had come before was immaterial. And she wasn't any of the women to whom he had made love before.

"I want to see," she said again.

And again, he shook his head.

She relented, but only because she didn't want to jeopardize the newfound intimacy they had discovered together. She told herself there would be other opportunities, that this night with Matthew would be the first of many. She wasn't the kind of woman to go for a one-night stand, and she assured herself that Matthew must realize that. If they made love tonight, it was because they were starting something new together.

There would be other times, she told herself again. Because she would prove to him tonight that she wasn't like other women.

Even so, she heard herself ask him, "How many other women have there been?"

She couldn't look him in the eye as she asked the question, and instead continued to gaze upon his wounded shoulder and her own fingers as they traced the edges of the scar. Matthew pulled her hand away. But where she feared he would return it to her side, instead he moved it to his mouth and pressed a gentle kiss to her palm.

"Not as many as you seem to think," he told her.

Rita did meet his gaze then, and she saw that he was telling her the truth. "I would have thought that a man like you..." she began.

But he halted her assessment by roping his arm around her waist and hauling her against him, covering her mouth with his once again. Rita went slack at the contact, so potent was the effect of his embrace. For long moments, she only stood limp in his arms, her hands pressed loosely against his shoulders, her legs tangled between his own. Her heart, though, pounded feverishly, rushing blood so quickly through her body that she almost grew dizzy. Then, suddenly, her body came alive, with need and demand and hunger. She wrapped her arms fiercely around Matthew's waist and returned his kiss with equal fire.

He groaned raggedly at her response, walking her backward, toward the living room she couldn't see. When they'd entered, she'd caught a glimpse of an elegantly appointed room with leather furniture and fine antiques surrounding a darkly colored Oriental rug. As she drew nearer, she noted a grandfather clock with its softly swaying pendulum, rows

of books on built-in shelves, and forest-green walls decorated with the occasional oil-on-canvas landscape. Expensive, refined, tasteful furnishings. Obviously, since Matthew Grayson was an expensive, refined, tasteful man.

He kept walking her backward until her legs bumped
against a leather-clad sofa the color of fine red wine. Rita
glanced toward the windows long enough to make sure the
curtains were closed, and reassured that they were, she lowered her hands to the fastenings of Matthew's trousers. As
she unzipped his fly, he opened his hands over her naked
back, then she tucked her fingers inside his pants.

She found him easily, so long and hard and ready was
he, and she covered the head of his shaft with her hand,
rubbing her palm over it in an indolent circle. Moisture
bloomed against her fingers as she touched him, making it
easier for her to glide her hand down the length of him. He
moaned against her mouth as she touched him, then moved
his hand down over her lace-covered fanny.

"You pulled your panties on over your garters," he murmured against her neck as he dropped his head to place a
series of soft, butterfly kisses there.

"I thought that was how you were supposed to do it,"
she murmured in reply, throwing her head back to make
herself more accessible to him.

"Only if you're planning to take the panties off and
leave the garters and stockings on," he told her.

"And isn't that what I should do?" she asked breathlessly.

He uttered another feral, erotic sound, then chuckled low.
"Oh, baby," he said, "you really know how to turn a man
on."

She did? Rita wondered. Well, that was certainly promising.

"Keep the shoes on, too," he added with a quick glimpse at her spiky heels.

She was going to ask why—that seemed so impractical after all—but the fire burning in his eyes gave her all the answer she needed. Matthew Grayson might be an expensive, refined, tasteful man, but he clearly enjoyed earthy, naughty, wanton sex. And something about the combination of the two made Rita want him all the more.

He hooked his fingers in the waistband of her panties and, without waiting for permission—not that Rita would have denied it—pushed them down over her hips and thighs. She stepped out of them easily and toed them aside, then returned to Matthew's arms. As she moved her hand back into his trousers and closed her fingers over him again, he slipped his hands beneath the silky garters and splayed them open over the soft lower curves of her naked fanny. Then he pulled her toward himself, and Rita rubbed her breasts languidly against the dark hair of his chest.

"I can't wait any longer," he told her. "I want to be inside you. Now, Rita. Let me make love to you now. Next time, I promise we'll go slower."

She nodded, then began pushing at his trousers. Together, they removed them, and Matthew urged her backward, down onto the couch. The sensation of smooth leather against her bare bottom was quite exquisite. As was the sensation of Matthew's gentle fingers when he moved them between her legs. Rita started to object, wanted to tell him she was ready for him *now,* but he deftly parted the soft, damp pleats of her flesh, then buried his fingers amid them, and she found that she couldn't say anything at all.

Again and again, he steered his hand expertly over her, each time delving more deeply along the furrows of those gentle folds. Rita cried out at the rush of erotic pleasure that wound through her in response to his touch, then instinctively parted her legs wider to facilitate his exploration. As he drove his tongue into her mouth again, he pushed a finger inside her delicate chasm, and she arched her body against him in reply, an action that only drove his digit deeper still, down to its very base. When she lowered herself again, his finger exited her, but before she had a chance to react, he pushed it into her again, penetrating her as deeply as before.

Once more, she bucked against him, and Matthew answered her by inserting two fingers inside her, splaying them wide at her entry before instigating a gentle in-and-out movement that nearly drove her mad. Every time he entered, Rita pushed her body against his marauding fingers, until the heated friction of the movement nearly undid her.

"You're so small," he whispered against her neck as he fingered her. "So tight. You haven't done this sort of thing very often, have you, Rita?"

Nearly insensate now with wanting him, all she could manage in reply was a feeble shake of her head and a raggedly gasped, "No."

She saw him smile at her response, as if the knowledge of her inexperience made him feel better. Then he kissed her deeply again. And as he kissed her, he moved his hand to the inside of her thigh, flattening his palm over her fevered flesh, pushing to open her legs more. Rita complied on instinct, bending her leg and dropping her foot to the floor. Matthew pushed the other leg against the side of the couch, bending that knee, too, and rising up on his own knees between them. He reached behind himself for a pillow then lifted Rita's hips so that he could tuck it beneath her, bringing her body closer to his surging erection. Then, gripping her hips in both hands, he moved forward, pushing the plump head of his member into her damp, eager opening.

She tilted her head back as she felt him entering her, loving the sensation of his hard shaft slipping easily into her saturated entrance. When he moved forward again, he pulled her hips toward him, and more of him pushed inside her, filling her. She gasped at a pinch of slight pain as he stretched her wider, then exhaled on a sigh of pleasure when she felt his hand close gently over her breast.

"How do you like it, Rita?" he asked her. "Slow or fast? Hard or gentle?"

Somewhere in her frenetic brain, she managed to comprehend what he was asking her, but she had no idea how to reply. She didn't know how she liked it, having never done it before. She'd heard it could be painful for a woman the first time, and she was already feeling a bit of discomfort due to Matthew's size, even though he hadn't even entered her all the way yet. The thought of him doing this slowly and gently made her think the pain would last longer. So maybe fast and hard was the way to go. The pain would be over with more quickly and then she could enjoy herself.

"Fast," she said weakly. "Hard. I want it fast and hard," she told him.

He grinned at that, a devilish, knowing kind of grin. "That's the way I like it, too," he told her. "Though there's something to be said for slow and easy in the right circumstances."

Tonight, however, he must not have considered the circumstances right for that, because before Rita had a chance to respond, he gripped her hips fiercely again and buried himself completely in her tender, very inexperienced, flesh. But not before hesitating over one small barrier he had to break to get there.

Rita cried out at the intensity of the pain that knifed through her at his penetration, and tears sprang to her eyes. Never had she imagined it would be like that, a pain so intense it nearly paralyzed her. Matthew immediately seemed to realize what had happened, because he quickly withdrew from her and pulled her up to a sitting position, facing him. For one long moment, he didn't say a word, only gazed at Rita as if he were very, very angry about something. Then his expression softened, and he lifted a hand to her face. Very gently, he thumbed tears first from one cheek, and then the other.

He still sounded stern, however, when he said, "Tell me this isn't your first time."

Rita feared he would change his mind about making love to her now that he knew of her uninitiated status—well, *previously* uninitiated status, at any rate. She was afraid that if she told him this was her first time, he would stop and ask her to get dressed and leave. And in spite of her earlier discomfort and distress, leaving was the last thing she wanted to do. She'd had a taste of what it could be like between a man and a woman—between Matthew and herself—and she wanted to learn the rest of it. All of it. The worst of it was over now, she told herself. She hadn't been prepared for him before, but now that she knew what to expect, it would be better. She was sure of it.

Still breathing raggedly from the fierceness of his initial entry, she asked, "What...what makes you think I...haven't...done this before?"

"Rita," he began, his tone pleading.

And then he began to set her away from him.

"No," she objected breathlessly, looping her arms around his neck to stop him. "Please, Matthew, don't stop. I want this. I want you to make love to me."

"But—"

"Please," she said again, hoping she didn't sound as desperate as she was beginning to feel. "Yes, it's my first time," she admitted. "But I don't want you to stop."

He studied her in silence for a moment longer, obviously torn over what he should do. Finally he said, "I don't want to hurt you."

She shook her head fiercely now. "You won't."

"I already have."

"The worst is over," she told him, certain that was true. "Just go slow this time. It'll be fine. Better than fine," she immediately corrected herself. "It'll be wonderful. Because you're wonderful. Please, Matthew," she pleaded one last time. "Make love to me."

He searched her face as if he were looking for the answer to some unanswerable question. Then, very slowly, he lifted his hand to her face again. Once more, he brushed away a tear, then he leaned forward and covered her mouth gently with his. As he kissed her, he moved her body toward his again, seating her in his lap, facing him. Then he looped her legs around his waist. She felt him at the heart of her womanhood, still hard and hot and ready for her. Once again he lifted her hips, then lowered her over his stiff shaft. But he went slowly this time, entering her with great care.

Rita gasped once at their first contact, but when she felt him tense, she relaxed her body and kissed him. "Keep going," she whispered against his mouth. "I'm all right."

"Are you sure?" he whispered back.

"Yes."

And she spoke the truth. Because never in her life had she felt more all right than she did in that moment.

Yes, there was still some discomfort, and yes, a little pain. But she was ready for it this time, and Matthew was holding her in a way that helped her better accommodate him. Little by little, he entered her more deeply, giving her time to adjust to him, time for her body to open more fully to receive him. By the time he was buried inside her again, as completely as he had been before, she felt full and happy and very aroused.

"Oh, that's better," she said as she circled one arm around his neck and the other around his shoulder. "So much better."

He, in turn, cupped his hands beneath her fanny, then lifted her slowly, withdrawing himself bit by bit. The slow friction of their bodies created a delicious heat, a heat that wound through Rita with an erotic sort of indolence. Again and again he moved their bodies that way, gradually accelerating the speed and the depth and the intensity. Soon, she forgot all about the initial pain she had experienced, because she was too busy feeling the exquisite pleasure of this new way of lovemaking.

A wild energy ignited in her midsection, spiraling outward into the rest of her body. And just when she thought it would circle into the cosmos, it shuddered and stuttered and halted, then exploded in a tumultuous commotion unlike anything she had ever felt before. Matthew's body went rigid at the same time hers did, and he spilled himself hotly inside her. For one long moment, they stilled, caught in each other's arms, and each other's climax. Then he slowly relaxed and fell backward against the sofa, pulling Rita down atop himself.

They lay entwined in silence for some moments, their bodies heated and slick with perspiration and their release. Rita pressed her cheek to Matthew's chest, loving the way he stroked his hands idly over her hair and the flesh of her back and shoulders. Beneath her ear, she could hear his heart pounding in a rapid, ragged rhythm that matched her own, and gently, she tented her hand over the place above it, as if wanting to protect it. She smiled when she realized how perfectly in sync the two of them were.

"Why didn't you tell me it was your first time?" she heard him say softly from above her.

She closed her eyes, not wanting to spoil this moment, but knowing he expected an answer. "Because I didn't think it would matter," she told him.

When he didn't reply to that, she lifted her head to look at him, and saw him gazing down at her in stunned disbelief. He stopped stroking her hair and fixed his gaze on hers. "You didn't think it would matter?" he echoed flatly.

Rita shook her head, then realized how what she had said might be misconstrued. She wanted to tell him it had mattered to *her,* of course, but that she hadn't thought it would be of any significance to *him.* She really hadn't thought it would make a difference to Matthew if this was her first time or her fourteenth.

He tilted his head back and expelled a soft sound of disappointment. "You didn't think it mattered," he echoed hollowly.

"No," she told him, still muzzy-headed and unable to articulate exactly what she wanted to say. "Not to you."

At that, his head snapped forward again, and he glared at her as if he couldn't believe what she had just said. "That's what kind of man you think I am?" he asked. "That something like this, with you, wouldn't matter to me?"

The vehemence in his voice surprised her. "Well, *did* it matter to you?" she asked, afraid to even hope.

He continued to study her with an expression she couldn't for the life of her identify. But instead of answering her question, he asked one of his own. "Do you actually have to ask me that?"

She eyed him curiously. "Well, I... Yes," she finally said. "I do."

He studied her in thoughtful silence for a long moment, then, very slowly, he began to nod. Somehow, Rita got the impression that he had drawn a conclusion of extreme importance, but she had no idea what that conclusion was.

"I see," was all he said.

"Matthew..." she began. But she honestly wasn't sure what she wanted to say to him.

Although, she thought further as she noted the way his eyes seemed to go hard and cold when he gazed back at her, maybe deep down she did know what she wanted to say to him. She was just afraid to say it. She didn't want to reveal that much of herself to him right now, not when she was feeling so vulnerable and so confused.

She still wasn't sure what had happened tonight, or why. She only knew she had experienced something she'd never experienced before, something profound and intimate and momentous and, yes, even life-changing. And she had shared it with a man for whom she had feelings, but they were feelings she wasn't able to identify or name. If she started trying to talk about this, she would make a mess of things, she knew. So she said nothing, only gazed back at him, hoping her uneasiness and bewilderment didn't show.

Hoping she was wrong about how he suddenly seemed to be growing more distant now than he had ever been before.

Matthew, however, seemed to know exactly what he was feeling and what he wanted to say, because he looked her squarely in the eye and told her, "I think you should go."

He might as well have thrown a glass of ice water in her face, so startled was Rita by the announcement. "But—" she began to object.

"Really, Rita," he continued as he disengaged himself

from her and stood, "I think it would probably be best if we called it a night." He didn't even bother to look for his briefs, only reached for his trousers and tugged them on, then switched all his focus on fastening them. "I guess we shouldn't have sent the driver off, after all. I can call you a cab, though."

By now Rita was so confused, she had no idea what to think. But she mimicked his movements as she spoke, rising from the couch to search for her dress, slipping it on over the garters and stockings she still wore, forsaking her bra and panties in her haste to simply get herself covered up.

"But...you said you would take me home," she said, knowing she sounded hurt and bewildered. But there was a good reason for that: She *was* hurt and bewildered. "Matthew, what are you talking about?" she continued. "What's going on?"

He crossed the living room to the foyer and picked up his shirt, shrugging it on, but leaving it unbuttoned. Not, however, before Rita got a look at the scars on the left side of his back. He was right—they were terrible. But she would have never, ever, found them repulsive. Because they were a part of Matthew. And he was beautiful to her. All of him.

When he spun around to look at her, he seemed to be suffering almost as much pain as she was herself. But how could that be possible, she wondered, when he was the one causing it?

"Get dressed," he said. "I'll call a cab." And then he spun on his heel and left her standing there alone.

More alone, in fact, than she had ever been in her life.

Rita had heard talk about the "wee, small hours of the morning," but she'd never really been a part of them before. Oh, she'd worked them for a while, when she'd been on third shift, but she'd always been so busy that she'd never had time to notice them. Certainly she'd never seen such hours from a social perspective. But as she gazed at the streets of Boston's North End from the back seat of her taxi, she realized that quite a few people were comfortable with this time of night. Plenty of bars and clubs were still going strong, and there were even a handful of people walking down the streets, presumably toward home. Or perhaps, she couldn't help thinking, toward a romantic, erotic tryst much like the one she had just enjoyed herself.

Until, of course, her lover had told her to leave.

Don't think about it, Rita, she told herself as she squeezed her eyes shut tight. *Just forget about what happened with Matthew.*

Heaven knew he'd probably already forgotten about it himself. He'd stayed wherever he'd gone until her cab arrived, then he'd returned to the living room long enough to show her the door. Literally. She still had no idea what she'd done wrong, but it must have been something terrible for him to have chilled toward her the way he had, so quickly and so completely. She'd hesitated at the front door before stepping through it, long enough to gaze up into his face one last time to see if she could understand what was going on inside his head. But he'd only looked back at her blankly, offering her not a single clue.

His shirt had still been hanging open, and, helpless to stop herself, Rita had lifted her hand toward his chest. Matthew had flinched and taken a step in retreat, then had offered her a crisp "Good night, Rita." She'd had no choice but to leave then. But she hadn't said a word in farewell.

She should just leave matters of sexual significance to the creatures of the night who knew how to handle them, she told herself now, gazing back out the window. It would be a long time before she ever ventured into something like that again.

When the cab pulled up in front of her brownstone, Rita reached for her purse to pay the driver. But he waved her off, assuring her his fee had been taken care of when the taxi was called. Then he drove off, leaving Rita standing on the curb, nonplussed. Matthew had paid for the cab that had taken her home after he'd thrown her out of his house, she reflected. She didn't know whether to be grateful or be even more offended. She settled on being even more confused.

All she wanted in that moment was to escape to her apartment and lock the door behind her—then maybe throw a few pieces of her heaviest furniture in front of it. Then she could cower like a wounded animal in the privacy of her home for the rest of the weekend and pretend she never had to go back to work again.

If she could just make it inside the brownstone without falling apart, she told herself, then she would be fine. The minute she cleared the front door, though, she intended to collapse into a quivering mass of self-doubt and self-recrimination.

Unfortunately, even that small consolation was going to have to wait, she realized once she was inside. Because there, in the receiving area of the brownstone—in the wee, small hours of the morning—sat her sister Maria and her cousin Emily. Maria was in her nightgown, a simple white cotton number, holding a cup of what was probably tea or cocoa. But Emily was still dressed in the same dress she had been wearing earlier at the party, a tailored, ivory-colored sheath. A matching jacket was slung over the arm of the chair where she sat. Her chin-length, dark-brown hair was pushed back from her face with a pearl-studded headband, and her brown eyes looked troubled. Her cup, Rita noted, sat neglected on the coffee table before her.

Immediately, alarm bells sounded in Rita's brain, and for a moment, anyway, she was able to put thoughts of Matthew Grayson and her colossal mistake out of her head. Something was obviously wrong. Both women wore expressions of concern, and they were both looking at Rita as if she had just interrupted a *very* serious conversation.

"What's wrong?" Rita demanded as she closed the door behind herself and strode quickly into the room. "What's happened?"

Maria quickly lifted a hand, palm out, in the halt position. "It's okay, Rita," she said quickly. "Everyone is fine."

Rita glanced at Emily, then back at her sister. "But…"

Emily expelled a soft sound of resignation. "I was out driving after the party, Rita, thinking about some things that have been bothering me, and I decided I needed to talk to someone. The brownstone was the closest Barone residence by then."

Plus, Rita knew, Emily and Maria had always been close.

"What's wrong?" she asked again as she covered the distance between herself and the other women, taking a seat on the opposite end of the sofa from Maria. "No one goes out driving in the middle of the night to think unless it's really, really important."

Emily sighed heavily, reached for the cup on the table before her, then changed her mind and leaned back into her chair again. "There's something going on at Baronessa," she said. "I can't put my finger on what, but something isn't right."

"What do you mean?" Rita asked.

But Emily only shook her head. "I probably shouldn't

have come here. I shouldn't have bothered you with this. It's silly. Just a feeling.''

"What kind of feeling?''

"Just..." Emily gave much thought to whatever she was trying to say, then gave up. "I don't know," she said, sounding helpless. "There's just...*something*...going on at Baronessa. Derrick's been acting kind of strangely lately, and I think he knows something he's not telling me. I came over here to see if maybe Maria had heard anything.''

Derrick, Emily's older brother, worked for Baronessa as the Vice President for Quality Assurance at the Brookline manufacturing plant. Emily was employed as his secretary. From all reports, the two made a good team, presumably because of their familiarity with each other and the rest of the Barones. Rita had never heard of there ever being a problem with either of them.

She turned to look at her sister, to see what Maria would say.

But Maria only shrugged. "I told Emily I can't think of anything. As far as I know, everything's business as usual. Well, as usual as it can be, considering recent events.''

"Like I said," Emily muttered, "I shouldn't have bothered you. It's silly. Especially now that I try to put voice to it.'' She sighed heavily. "I shouldn't have come. I'm sorry to have woken you up, Maria.''

Maria waved off her concern and enjoyed a generous sip from her mug. "Don't worry about it, Emily. I was awake anyway.''

Emily eyed her cousin with much consideration. "I thought you seemed awfully awake when you answered the door in the middle of the night. What are *you* losing sleep over?''

Rita turned to look at her sister, too. "That reminds me. There's something I've been wanting to ask you.''

Maria looked vaguely alarmed by the statement. "What?" she asked warily.

"You've been spending an awful lot of time away from home lately," Rita said. "Much more than you used to. And at night, too, when you always used to be home."

Now Maria looked *definitely* alarmed. "I, ah… I've, um… Well… It's just that…" She swallowed with some difficulty and darted her gaze away from Rita's.

This ought to be good, Rita thought. Maria was the worst liar on the planet. She could never look at someone straight on when she was about to tell a fib.

"There's just, um," Maria began again, "there's, ah…there's just been a lot of work lately. At the gelateria, I mean," she added hastily, "what with the botched launch of the passionfruit flavor and this new contest, I've been putting in a lot more hours than usual."

Rita nodded, not believing a word of it. "I think you've got a guy," she announced flatly.

Maria's olive complexion flushed. "I—I—I have no idea what you mean," her sister stammered.

Rita and Emily exchanged looks, then both began to laugh, something that surprised Rita. She wouldn't have thought she could manage such a thing after the evening she'd had. But maybe teasing her sister was what she needed to take her mind off her own troubles with Matthew.

"You do, don't you?" she charged Maria. "You have a guy you've been seeing. And you don't want the rest of us to know about it."

"No, it isn't that," Maria objected vehemently.

Too vehemently, Rita thought. "C'mon, Maria, you're the worst liar on the planet and you know it. What's his name?"

Her sister's gaze darted from Rita to Emily and back again. For a moment, she looked utterly miserable. Then, suddenly, she smiled. Instead of revealing the name of her guy, though, she only said, "He's really wonderful. You'd both like him."

"Then why don't you bring him around?" Emily asked. "We'd all love to meet him."

Now Maria's smile fell. "Oh, I can't. He's, um, shy," she finally finished. "Yeah, that's it. He's shy. And you know how overwhelming the Barones can be."

Boy, did Rita know that. She'd spent a good part of this evening wondering how she was going to make Matthew feel comfortable within the Barone fold.

Dammit, she thought. Was she *ever* going to be able to think about anything again without Matthew wandering into the equation?

"Shy, huh?" she said, not bothering to hide her doubt. "Something tells me there's a little more to it than that." She sighed. "But I won't press you for details. And I promise not to say a word to anyone else. Emily does, too," she added with a quick glance at her cousin for confirmation, a glance that Emily returned with an affirming nod. "I figure you'll bring him around when you're ready," Rita added. "Especially if he means enough to you that the mere mention of him makes you blush the way you do."

She smiled when her sister blushed again. But her smile fell when she heard Maria's question.

"So what about *your* guy?" her sister asked. "You and the yummy Dr. Grayson looked pretty chummy this evening." She turned a meaningful gaze to the clock on the mantel. "And it's awfully late for you to be getting in," she added. "And is that your bra I see peeking out of your purse?"

Panicked, Rita glanced down at her purse, only to find that it was perfectly fine.

"Gotcha!" Maria said with a laugh.

When Emily joined in, Rita had no choice but to chuckle, too.

"So you admit your bra is in your purse?" Maria asked, still laughing.

"I admit no such thing," Rita said. "It was just a reflex."

"Mmm-hmm," Maria murmured. "If you say so. I won't ask about any other reflexes you might have had tonight."

Good, Rita thought. Because her reflexes tonight were the last thing she wanted to think about. She dipped her head toward the cup her sister held. "Is there any more of whatever that is?" she asked, hoping it was cocoa, because as everyone knew, chocolate was the universal comfort food.

Maria glanced down into her mug. "Chianti? Sure. We're Italian, Rita, remember? There's always room for Chianti."

Rita laughed again, and somehow, in doing so, some of the tension in her body eased. Now if she could just do something about the tension in her mind, her spirit and her emotions, she'd be just fine. Chianti sounded like a very good idea. That, coupled with a long soak in the tub—and a weekend barricaded in her apartment with heavy furniture pushed against the door—sounded like just the thing she needed. Eventually, she knew, she'd have to start thinking about Monday morning and seeing Matthew Grayson again. But she'd think about that later, she promised herself.

Probably on Monday morning.

Seven

Monday morning, Matthew reflected morosely as he gazed out his office window at the hazy gray drizzle falling on the other side. A rainy Monday morning, at that. How appropriate, as the weather reflected his mood. Actually his feelings were much more turbulent than the patter of rain that softly pelted his window.

With a muttered oath, he turned his back on the rain and paced the entire length of his office. Then he spun around and paced back to the window again. He had promised himself that by Monday morning, he would have done one of two things: Either he would have written off what had happened with Rita Barone on Friday night as One of Those Things and then forgotten about it, or else he would have thought of some way to explain to her why he had behaved like such an ass, offered her an apology, and then forgotten about it.

Unfortunately his deadline was now upon him, and neither of those things had happened. There was no way Matthew could ever casually write off what had happened with Rita Barone, because he cared far too much about her. And his appalling behavior of Friday night defied explanation.

He had just been so stunned by her assessment of him, that he hadn't known how to react. She had honestly thought him an unfeeling enough cad not to even care that she—Rita Barone, the object of his secret admiration—had made him her first lover. Even after the explosive way the two of them had come together, she had thought him so devoid of emotion that he wouldn't consider what had happened important. She had thought him that heartless and uncaring.

Which meant that, in spite of her assertion to the contrary, she thought him a beast. Just like everyone else at Boston General. She hadn't thought he was capable of caring for another human being, when in fact what he felt for her was—

He didn't want to think about that now, hadn't allowed himself to think about it. Not long enough to understand what it meant, at any rate. All he'd been able to think about for the entire weekend, all he'd been able to hear in his head, again and again, was the question she'd asked him.

Well, did *it matter to you?*

She hadn't been able to tell, he thought now. Even after what the two of them had done, what the two of them had shared, she hadn't been able to sense how he felt about her. She hadn't realized he—

Maybe he really was a beast, after all, Matthew thought, interrupting his own thoughts before they could get carried away and venture into territory he'd just as soon not visit right now. He must be a beast, because why else would he have reacted the way he had that night? Only a beast would have behaved in such a way.

He shouldn't have told her to leave, and he shouldn't have called a cab to make her leaving easier. His stomach still clenched into a cold fist at the memory of how he had done that. Never in his life had he behaved like such a heel toward a woman. But he hadn't been thinking. He had acted out of anger and fear. He'd been angry that Rita had been so ready to believe him heartless, and he'd been afraid of what he might say—or, worse, what he might reveal—if he had allowed her to stay. And now...

He expelled another frustrated growl and drove both hands into his hair, then went back to pacing like a caged animal. Now Rita probably wouldn't let him come near her to explain, he thought, even if he had any idea what to say. And, frankly, he couldn't blame her.

He halted by the window again, gazing down into the dreary street below. From his office, he could see the employee entrance to the hospital, and he was watching, as he often did on rainy days, for the arrival of a bright yellow umbrella. Under that bright yellow umbrella would be Rita Barone, he knew. Everyone else favored black umbrellas, more suitable to the mood of the weather. Not Rita. Hers suited her own sunny nature. Within moments of beginning his search, Matthew found his quarry. Six fifty-five, he noted when he glanced down at his watch. As reliable as a finely tuned clock was Rita Barone.

He wished he could say the same about his emotions.

Either write off what happened, Grayson, or explain your behavior and apologize, he told himself again. *Which is it going to be?*

One way or another, he needed to send a signal to Rita Barone. He had to let her know where the two of them stood. He just wished he knew exactly where that was.

They worked together, he reminded himself. They would inevitably be seeing each other, regularly at that. How were they supposed to be comfortable doing that after what had happened Friday night?

They wouldn't be comfortable, he answered himself immediately, not unless they came to terms with it. But just what, he wondered, were those terms going to be?

Rita felt edgy and hyperaware of her surroundings as she took her seat at the nurses' station in CCU Monday morning. She felt dizzy and disoriented from a lack of sleep—a quick calculation told her she'd managed to achieve roughly six nanoseconds of shut-eye this weekend—and her head was pounding.

It had only been once she was safely ensconced in her own bed Friday night—or, rather, Saturday morning—with the covers pulled up to her chin, that she had realized something very, very important: She and Matthew had neglected to use any sort of birth control when they'd made love. They'd both been so carried away by what was happening—so stunned and unprepared—that neither had given a second thought to what should have been their primary concern.

Some health professional she was, Rita thought. Some fast figuring had reassured her—sort of—that the timing was all wrong for her to have gotten pregnant, but she was shaken by her carelessness. Yes, it had been her first time, but that wasn't any excuse for not taking precautions. Mother Nature didn't care how many times you copulated before conceiving, only that all the biological mechanics were intact and running on schedule.

Fortunately, Rita's biological mechanics ran like clockwork, which meant she wasn't in danger of getting pregnant. Unfortunately, though, her emotional mechanics weren't nearly so reliable. Which meant she was in danger of being hurt.

She told herself to forget about what had happened Friday night and put it down to one of those stupid mistakes all women are entitled to make once in their lives. Once, she repeated emphatically to herself. She had learned something in making that mistake, and she would use that knowledge in the future to make sure she didn't make other mistakes like it. She would guard her heart more carefully, and she would not fall so easily into a situation like that again. Especially not with a man like Matthew Grayson, who could, quite literally, be making love to a woman one minute and calling a cab for her the next.

Now, her head was really throbbing, and her stomach was upset, too, because her breakfast had consisted of nothing more than two cups of coffee and three buffered aspirins. Maybe when the dietary aides brought up breakfast for the patients, they'd have an extra tray.

"Rita."

At the sound of Matthew's voice uttering her name so quietly, she went liquid all over. She really wasn't ready to see him yet. She wouldn't be ready for at least another century or two. Or ten.

With much reluctance, she turned in her chair to face him, and remembering what had happened the last time she'd done that, she stood up before her thoughts could get carried away. Then she realized that, thanks to Friday night, her thoughts about Matthew Grayson were going to include sexually explicit images for some time now. She wondered how long it would be before they started to fade.

Then she gazed up into his dreamy green eyes, noted the fine chestnut hair she had twined so lovingly in her fingers, saw the scars on his face that she had touched with such care, and she knew there would never be a day when she didn't think about him with a heavy heart and wonder what might have been. He was dressed in another one of his dark, sexy power suits, but had forsaken his white doctor jacket today. All in all, he looked wonderful and irresistible and she wanted very much to kiss him.

Instead, she mustered a professional voice and replied, "Yes, Dr. Grayson?"

He flinched a little at her use of the formal title, but recovered quickly. "Do you have a moment?" he asked, clearly finding it as difficult as she to remain businesslike.

She scrambled for excuses. "Actually," she said, "I'm pretty strapped for time. It's always this way after the weekend. I have a lot of catching up to do."

"It will only take a moment," he told her.

She bit her lip to keep herself from retorting with something like, *Oh, you mean like Friday night did?* That would only serve to make them both even more uncomfortable than they already were. And it would let Matthew know how much she was still hurting. The last thing she wanted was for him to think she cared about him as much as she did. Especially when he didn't return the feeling.

"Really, I'm just swamped," she told him dispassionately. "Maybe another time."

He glanced down at the place where she had been sitting—the totally tidy, completely uncluttered place where she had been sitting. The place where nothing seemed even to be happening, let alone swamping her. Likewise incriminating was the fact that her mail slot only had what appeared to be one memo inside it.

Damn. Of all the weekends for the CCU to be uneventful, she thought.

She blew out a halfhearted sigh. "All right," she conceded without looking at him, pretending to smooth out a nonexistent wrinkle on the shirt of her blue scrubs. "You may have a moment."

"Thank you," he replied. But she could tell it was taking a lot for him to remain unaffected.

She hadn't really thought he would tell her whatever he wanted to tell her there at the nurses' station—shift changes meant twice as many people as usual milling about—but Rita still flinched when Matthew's arm skimmed her shoulder as he gestured her forward. Even that small physical contact with him made her feel as if he'd struck a spark against her.

Obediently, however, she made her way forward, pausing only long enough to let him catch up since he was the one who knew where they were going. He ducked his head into the CCU waiting room as they passed it, but there were two people in there sleeping, so he continued on his way, as did Rita. Finally, he tugged on the door to a supply closet and, ever the gentleman, stood aside for her to enter first. She shook her head as she did, flicking on the light switch as she went. Matthew followed, letting the door swing closed behind him. Then it was just the two of them. And a couple hundred rolls of gauze and toilet paper.

What a romantic interlude this was going to be, she thought wryly. Then again, considering the way she felt, gauze and toilet paper might both come in handy.

She lifted her wrist and eyed her watch meaningfully. "Your moment begins now," she said coolly.

"Rita," Matthew began.

But in spite of his assurance that he wouldn't waste her time, he said nothing more after that. When she glanced up from her watch, she saw him gazing at her with what looked like a mixture of anguish and longing, and the coldness toward him she had nurtured all weekend suddenly began to thaw. She told herself not to warm to him, to remember the way he had acted Friday and not focus on his reaction to her now. If he was anguished, it was probably only because he feared she was going to make his working life difficult. And if he was longing for something, it was doubtless for things to go back to the way they were a week ago. Before they had made such a colossal blunder.

Finally, though, he said, in a rush of words so fast she missed most of them, "I'm sorry about the way I acted Friday night."

She arched her brows in both surprise and query. "What?" she said. "You're what?"

He expelled an impatient breath, but his eyes never left hers as he repeated, more clearly, "I'm sorry. About the way I acted. Friday night," he concluded uneasily.

She really hadn't expected him to apologize. She had expected him to offer up some lame excuse, and then tell her they should both just try and forget about it and pretend nothing had happened. An apology, though...

Maybe, she thought, there was hope for him, for *them*, yet.

"But I think we probably should both just try and forget about it and pretend nothing happened," he added.

Her heart sank. So much for hope. So much for him. So much for *them*.

It really hadn't meant anything to him, she realized. After the way he had been acting this morning, she had begun to think maybe she had been wrong about what had happened Friday night, and that he wasn't like most men. She had thought that maybe it really had meant something to him, the fact that he had been her first. But now he wanted to brush it off and pretend it had never happened.

Obviously it *hadn't* mattered. Not to him.

"Fine," she said shortly. Even though *fine* was the last thing she was feeling. "Is that it?" She glanced down at her watch again. "Wow, it really did just take a moment. You're good, Dr. Grayson."

Immediately she wished she hadn't uttered that last sarcastic sentiment. One sarcastic sentiment would have been plenty, but no, she'd had to push too hard. That was Rita. Just like a Barone, always overdoing it.

"Now, if you'll excuse me," she said miserably.

Damn, she felt the sting of tears welling in her eyes. The last thing she needed was for Matthew Grayson to see her crying. So she spun quickly around and headed for the door. She realized too late that he stood between her and it, and as she tried to push him aside so that she could make her escape, he snaked out his hand and circled loose fingers around her wrist, effectively stopping her in her place.

"Rita," he said again.

"What?" she replied tersely without turning around.

"I really am sorry."

She jerked her wrist free and reached for the door and pulled it open. But he flattened his hand against it and pushed it closed again. She was afraid to turn around, afraid to look at him, because she feared she would start crying if she did. So she only stood still, gazing at the closed door, mentally willing him to move his hand so she could make her escape.

Instead, he moved closer to her, coming to a halt immediately behind her, close enough that she could smell the fresh, clean scent of him and feel the heat of his body mingling with her own. His breath stirred her hair, and if she closed her eyes, she fancied she could detect the beating of his heart in sync with her own.

"Do you accept my apology?" he asked softly.

She nodded slowly, trying to keep herself on kilter, but the world still felt as if it were spinning out of control beneath her feet. "Yes," she told him. "I accept your apology." And she did. Even if she couldn't accept much else.

He still had his hand pressed against the door, but she thought she saw his fingers relax some.

"Then you agree we should just forget about Friday night and pretend it never happened?" he asked her.

She nodded again, even though she knew she was lying when she agreed with him. So she continued to keep her back to him when she replied, "Yes, we should just forget about it. We're both adults, and we can be mature about this. It was one of those things. Too much champagne, too much partying. We got a little carried away. It could have happened to anyone."

Except that it hadn't happened to anyone, she thought further. It had happened to her. And things like that didn't happen to Rita Barone. Not unless there was a good reason for it. And not without repercussions. Now if she could only figure out what that good reason was, and what those repercussions might be. Then maybe she could start to make some sense of it all. And maybe she could move on with her life.

And maybe, she thought further, while she was sleeping tonight, leprechauns would come into her room and dance the merengue by the light of the moon.

"Excuse me," she said again. "But I have to go to work."

For a moment, she didn't think Matthew was going to move his hand. And for that same moment, she thought he was going to move his body closer to hers. She tensed as she waited to see what he would do, then was almost disappointed when he removed his hand from the door to let her leave. Deep down, she had been hoping he would touch her, she realized. But then, why would he do that, when all he wanted was to forget about her?

Without another word, Rita reached for the door and tugged it open. Somehow, she managed to keep her composure as she strode through it and back to the nurses' station. She maintained that composure as she collected patient files and studied their requirements for the day. In fact, once Matthew left the area, she was able to focus entirely on her work and complete her job in the same fashion she always did, caring for her patients.

It never ceased to amaze her, she thought as she treated the people in CCU that day, what the human heart was capable of surviving.

She had agreed with him.

Matthew retreated to his office at the end of his morning rounds, slumped into the chair behind his desk, spun it around to gaze out at the rain and felt more empty than he'd ever felt in his life. After seeing more than two dozen patients, some of them in critical condition, all he could think about was Rita Barone, and how she had gazed at him so coolly, then turned her back on him and agreed that they should just forget about what had happened Friday night.

But, then, what the hell had he expected? he demanded of himself. How else would a woman react to a man who had almost literally thrown her out of his house after making love to her, without explanation, without so much as a fare-thee-well? Matthew was lucky she was speaking to him at all. Had he thought she would fall to her knees and beg him to give their relationship a second chance? They didn't even have a relationship to give a second chance to, because he'd ruined the chance for one to start.

He leaned his head back against his chair. Oh, who was he kidding? A relationship? Between beautiful, bubbly Rita Barone and the Beast of Boston General? Yeah, right.

And now she wasn't even wearing the pin or bracelet

he'd given her. He couldn't even enjoy his private thrill of
that secret closeness to her anymore.

He wished he knew why she'd ended what had been a
tradition for months now. She'd liked the gifts. He knew
that. So why had she stopped wearing them? And how
could he find an answer when he dared not ask her himself,
or risk revealing his identity as the giver?

Now more than ever before, such a discovery would
prove disastrous. It was bad enough being Matthew Grayson, MD, the Beast of Boston General. If anyone found out
he was Rita Barone's secret admirer, he'd become Matthew
Grayson, MD, the laughingstock of Boston General. He'd
been a laughingstock before. He hadn't liked it, and didn't
want to be one again.

Forget about it, he told himself. Forget about all of it.
Forget about Rita Barone. Forget that you ever left her a
gift. Forget you ever had a crush on her at all.

If only it were that easy. But something told him he'd
never be able to banish her from his thoughts completely.
Because in making love to her, he had allowed her to become a part of himself. And he was beginning to suspect
that it was a part, like his heart, that he wouldn't be able
to live without.

In the two weeks that followed her official breakup with
Matthew—even though, deep down, she had to acknowl-
edge that one couldn't break up a relationship one never
had to begin with—Rita did everything she could to avoid
seeing him. She switched shifts with other nurses, gladly
taking on the graveyard shift she had once been so grateful
to leave behind. She traded off units with other nurses in
an effort to remove herself from CCU, but that only landed
her in spots she didn't much care to visit—like neonatal,
surrounded by babies, and the all-too-real reminder of what

could be waiting for her in her near future, thanks to her carelessness. Fortunately, barely a week passed before she discovered there was no danger of her being pregnant. Strangely, though, when her period did arrive, she experienced an odd sort of melancholy about it.

She told herself she was crazy to be disappointed she hadn't gotten pregnant from her one-night stand with the beastly Dr. Matthew Grayson. But for some reason, the thought of having his child wasn't nearly as off-putting as she might have thought it would be. Of course, it would have helped enormously if Matthew was around to share in the blessed event, she would then remind herself brutally. That wasn't likely, since he'd grown tired of her within moments of making love to her.

No, she was better off free of Matthew Grayson, she assured herself.

After two weeks of avoiding him, however, Rita had no choice but to accept the fact that she was only putting off the inevitable. Short of a permanent transfer to another unit, or another hospital, she wasn't going to be able to escape Matthew. She would simply have to make the best of working alongside him, in spite of what had happened. After all, what had happened *wasn't* going to happen again, she vowed steadfastly.

She would just have to face the fact that she had given herself—her heart—to a man who couldn't possibly appreciate what it meant to have it, and then she would have to move on with her life. And she would just have to be more careful the next time she fell in love.

Oh, dear, she thought when that realization sprang into her head one very snowy morning in late April. Was that really what had happened? she wondered. Was that what was at the root of all of this? Had she honestly fallen in love with the beastly Dr. Grayson?

She thought about that for a moment as she stood in the hospital cafeteria, sipping a cup of mid-morning coffee and watching a thick curtain of snow through the windows. She had barely managed to make it to work before the storm had become nearly impenetrable. The weather forecasters said the late-season nor'easter was only going to get worse before it got better. But, then, that was spring in New England. Mild and sunny one day, blustery and stormy the next. And always unpredictable.

Much like Matthew Grayson, she couldn't help thinking. *Had* she fallen in love with him?

As Rita sipped her coffee and stared out at the snow, she began to think that maybe, just maybe, she had.

She was in love with Matthew Grayson. She had given her heart to a man who didn't want it. A beast, she told herself. Everyone at the hospital had always said so.

Immediately, though, she took exception to her own assertion. Deep down, she knew Matthew wasn't a beast at all. She never would have fallen in love with him if he had been. During that one evening the two of them had spent together, he hadn't been beastly in any way. No, he'd been quite charming. Kind, attentive, passionate. Until the end anyway. So why had he reverted to his old beastly self then?

Rita turned her back on the weather that so reminded her of Matthew Grayson and decided not to think about it. Not to think about him or about what had happened. She needed to forget about it, move on. She only wished she knew where she would end up.

When she returned to the nurses' station, it was with a feeling of foreboding. She didn't know if it was due to the ferocious weather raging outside, or the tumultuous emotions roaring inside her. But when she glanced into her mail slot, as she habitually did when she'd been away from the

nurses' station for any length of time, the feeling only mul-
tiplied. Because there, tied with a gold ribbon, lay, not a
white package this time, but a perfect, apricot-colored
sweetheart rose.

Rita's first instinct was to glance around the unit, to see
if there were any dark, shadowy figures lurking about. Naturally, though, she saw no one. In fact, the unit was surprisingly deserted, something that only made her feel more
apprehensive. Some of the nurses had taken an early lunch,
she knew, and the others were doubtless checking on patients or conferring with doctors. Some hadn't made it in
at all, thanks to the weather. But in that moment, as Rita
gazed down at the rose, she'd never felt more alone in her
life.

Reluctantly, she reached for the flower, pulling it out of
her mail slot and holding it up to her nose. Closing her
eyes, she inhaled deeply of its tangy fragrance, an almost
narcotic scent that evoked too many pleasurable sensations
for her to handle in her emotionally fragile state. So she
opened her eyes again, lowering the rose some, tracing the
perfect, silky petals one by one.

Because of the gold ribbon tied around the stem, she
knew the rose was from her secret admirer. Or perhaps her
stalker. She honestly didn't know for sure. But why today?
she wondered. And why a rose? It wasn't something he
could wrap in his traditional white paper. And it certainly
wasn't a special occasion of any kind.

Well, not to her secret admirer, at any rate, Rita thought.
Though it was the two-week anniversary of the night she
had made love with Matthew. Not that she was counting
or anything, and not that she was commemorating it.

She lifted a trembling hand to her forehead, rubbing at
a headache that seemed to erupt out of nowhere. This was
crazy, she told herself. She had to find out who was doing

this. She wasn't going to be able to relax until she did. As much as she tried to reassure herself that there was nothing nefarious behind the gifts, she couldn't quite convince herself of their harmlessness. Until she knew the truth, she wasn't going to feel safe or content at work anymore.

She had to laugh derisively at that. It wasn't just her secret admirer preventing her from enjoying her work anymore. It was the presence of Matthew Grayson, too.

Expelling a soft sound of frustration, Rita set the rose down on the nurses' station and tried not to think about her admirer *or* Matthew. Somehow, though, she knew it was going to be a long time before either of them stopped being a concern.

Eight

By the time Rita's shift ended at three o'clock, the storm had picked up enough speed and strength that a weather advisory was in full effect. No one was supposed to attempt travel unless it was a medical emergency. But Rita didn't want to remain at the hospital when her friendly neighborhood stalker might be lurking about.

He's not a stalker, she tried to tell herself again as she pushed open the door to the changing room and made her way to her locker.

She gazed at the sweetheart rose again, then placed it gingerly on the bench. It was truly spectacular, a perfect blossom in every sense of the word, more beautiful than anything the human hand could ever hope to manufacture. And somehow, it was made even more poignant by the presence of the storm outside. It was a breath of spring, an image of hopefulness and renewal, in the midst of an icy, bitter tempest. For that reason, if no other, she wanted to take good care of it.

And hey, even if the bearer of the rose didn't realize it, it had arrived on a special day. Special to Rita, anyway. Even if Matthew had probably forgotten all about it by now.

Two weeks, she marveled as she tugged her scrubs shirt over her head and stuffed it into the duffel bag. Had it really only been that long? In many ways, it seemed as if she'd lived a lifetime since making love with Matthew. And in many ways, she felt like a completely different person. But it had only been two weeks. Two weeks of trying to avoid him when she could, and pretending everything was fine when she couldn't. Two weeks of seeing those dreamy green eyes, and smelling that spicy fragrance he wore, and occasionally—accidentally, of course—brushing up against him in the close confines of the nurses' station or one of the crowded rooms. Two weeks of remembering the ways he had touched her and kissed her and filled her. Two weeks of feeling lonelier and more empty than she'd ever felt in her life. But her stalker/admirer couldn't know that, she told herself, pushing her melancholy ruminations away.

Who could it be? she wondered again. Thanks to the weather, the hospital was fairly deserted today. There had been few visitors, and staff was short. Had she not just worked a double shift herself, she would have been drafted into staying for another one. But she was exhausted as it was, and would probably do more harm than good. It would be better if she went home. Not only to rest, but to put some distance between herself and whoever had left the rose for her.

Quickly, she finished changing out of the scrubs she'd been wearing for nearly eighteen hours, and reached for the heavy clothes that would keep her warm as she struggled to walk home through weather better suited to polar bears. Then she gathered up her duffel bag, leaving the rose sitting on the bench.

She should leave it for someone else to find, she thought. Someone who would appreciate it for its simple beauty and not consider it a symbol of something potentially sinister. Besides, it would probably never survive the storm outside.

She took a step away, then immediately changed her mind. She didn't know why, but she wanted to keep the rose with her. So she picked it up again and tucked it carefully inside her shearling jacket, patting the thick fabric gently as she strode toward the locker-room door.

She had exited the hospital through the employee entrance and was wrestling with her mittens when a tall, solid body came to a halt beside hers. She glanced up, squinting against the cold wind that whipped snow up even under the protective awning, only to find Matthew Grayson gazing down at her.

He was dressed for the elements, too, only much more fashionably than she. His camel-colored overcoat was obviously cashmere, as was the Stewart tartan scarf folded neatly around his neck and tucked tidily into his lapels. His brown leather gloves looked butter-soft and smooth, and, somehow, he even made a brown, cuffed knit cap look elegant. Try as she might, Rita couldn't take her eyes off him. Funnily enough, he didn't seem to be able to take his eyes off her, either.

For one long moment, they only stood there, gazing at each other in silence, neither moving so much as an inch, as if they'd been frozen in place by the elements. Snow swirled up around them from the sidewalk below, spiraling and sparkling around them like fine, enchanted fairy dust. Finally, though, Matthew spoke, breaking the spell, making

Rita feel as if she had tumbled into a dream and back out again, more disoriented than before.

"You're not planning to walk home in this," he said.

She shrugged uneasily as she squinted at the flying snow. "I don't have much choice."

"It's fifteen blocks," he pointed out unnecessarily.

Rita opened her mouth to tell him she'd be fine, then stopped, eyeing him narrowly. "How do you know it's fifteen blocks to my house?" she asked. "You don't know where I live."

He reared his head back at that, looking uncomfortable. But his reply was utterly innocent, and his tone of voice bland. "I have the addresses and phone numbers of everyone in CCU," he told her. "Just in case."

In case of what? she wanted to ask. Then she told herself she was being overly suspicious. It made perfect sense that Matthew would want to be able to contact anyone in the unit about a patient or some other hospital matter. This whole stalker/admirer business had her jumping at shadows.

"I'm sorry," she apologized. "I'm just a little edgy. The weather," she said lamely.

He nodded. "All the more reason for you not to try and make it home," he told her.

"Well, I can't stay here all night," she said, nodding toward the hospital behind her.

"Why not?" he asked. "There's food, coffee, beds, heat, TV," he concluded the list with a smile, "everything you need to battle the inclement weather."

"Oh, sure," she agreed wryly. "Cafeteria food, bad coffee, hospital beds and no premium channels. And the heat can be iffy," she added. "Plus, I might run into someone I don't want to run into."

His expression and posture changed drastically at her

comment, going from uneasy armistice to vague hostility. "No, you won't," he told her flatly. "In case you've forgotten, it's only a couple of blocks to my house. I'm going home. You'll be perfectly fine here."

Only then did Rita realize that Matthew thought she was talking about him. "No, I didn't mean that," she hastily corrected herself. She even went so far as to extend her hand toward him, cupping her mittened hand lightly over his forearm to reassure him. "I wasn't talking about you, Matthew. I was talking about my stalker."

Then she squeezed her eyes shut tight at what she'd revealed and how she must have sounded. She hoped he didn't think her a paranoid psychotic harboring delusions of persecution?

"Stalker?" he echoed incredulously. "What are you talking about?"

"Well, he may not be a stalker," she quickly backpedaled. "I don't know what he is. But he makes me... uncomfortable. And I don't want to risk running into him on a dark and stormy afternoon when the hospital is deserted and no one will be around to hear my impotent cries for help."

He gazed at her without comprehension. "I'm sorry, but I still have no idea what you're talking about."

Rita blew out a long, impatient breath, and told him, with profound understatement, "It's a long story."

He gazed back at her for some time without speaking, as if he were weighing a matter of grave consequence. Then, softly, and not a little uncertainly, he said, "Why don't you come to my place instead of going home?"

Rita's eyebrows shot up to the edge of her beret in surprise. "I—I—I—" she stammered. "I—I'm not sure that's such a good idea. Thanks, anyway."

He expelled a frustrated sound. "Look, I'm not expecting anything to happen, okay? I just meant it's closer than your place, and if you're not comfortable staying here at the hospital, it might be a better alternative. And then I wouldn't sit around worrying about whether you made it home in this storm.''

"Thanks," Rita said again, "but I don't think—"

"Rita," he interjected, his tone of voice mild, but firm. "Nothing will happen. I promise. I'm suggesting this as one friend to another. I hope we are, at least, still that.''

She said nothing in response to that, not sure she trusted her voice not to conceal her true feelings. Friends with Matthew Grayson? After what the two of them had shared? She'd never done that with any of her other friends, and something told her she wasn't likely to. He was much more to her than a friend, she knew. But there was no reason she had to reveal that to him.

"I have an extra bedroom," he continued in that same innocuous, matter-of-fact voice, "and if you want to barricade yourself inside it and pretend I don't exist, that's fine. I'll slip you some lettuce leaves under the door so you won't starve," he added with a tentative smile.

It wasn't a good idea, Rita thought. It really, really wasn't a good idea. There were reports that the storm was only going to get worse, which meant she could be stranded at Matthew's place for a lot longer than just tonight. But when she turned her gaze again to the churning snow, she saw that it was nearly opaque past the steps leading down to the sidewalk.

Still, could she accept his suggestion? Being alone with Matthew, feeling the way she did about him, she would doubtless say or do something she shouldn't. And then she'd feel even worse than she already did.

"Besides," he added, his voice turning serious again, "I want to hear about this stalker of yours.''

"Well, he may not be a stalker," she said. "He may just be a secret admirer."

Matthew's expression went completely slack at that, and his lips parted slightly, as if he wanted to say something, but didn't know what. "Secret admirer?" he finally echoed, his voice sounding hollow and cold.

"That's what most of the nurses think he is," Rita told him. "I mean, you've probably heard the rumors, right? They've been going around since Valentine's Day."

"Valentine's Day?" he echoed again, still sounding a little stunned.

Rita nodded. "That's when the first anonymous gift showed up in my mail slot at the nurses' station in CCU. That little bandaged heart pin I used to wear on my scrubs all the time. Maybe you noticed it?"

"Bandaged heart pin?" Matthew repeated like a parrot, his expression still devoid of any identifiable emotion.

She nodded again, more slowly this time, thinking his reaction was kind of odd. "Yeah," she said. "And then he left me another anonymous gift on my birthday. A charm bracelet that I also used to wear until recently."

"Charm bracelet?"

"Uh-huh. And then, a few weeks ago, on the anniversary of the day I started working at the hospital, he left me a third anonymous gift. A crystal heart paperweight."

"Crystal heart paperweight?"

"Yeah," Rita said. Matthew really was acting weird, repeating everything she said like a wind-up toy. "It was really beautiful, but it was much more expensive than the first gifts. And it made me feel kind of…creepy."

"Creepy?"

"Uh-huh. And then today, just a couple of hours ago, in fact, he left me a rose. At least, I think it was him who left it. But today isn't a special occasion. Well, not to my stalker, anyway," she quickly corrected herself before she could stop herself.

But not before Matthew caught her implication. Because suddenly, he was completely tuned into what she was saying, his eyes fixed on hers, his mouth set in a firm, tight line. He, too, realized the significance of the date. He was thinking about two Fridays ago, just as she was.

"Come home with me, Rita," he said again, with more conviction this time.

"Matthew, I'm not sure it's—"

"Come home with me."

And there was something in his voice when he said it that time that made her reconsider. Maybe she should go home with him, she thought. Maybe now that they'd put a little distance between themselves and that night, they could talk about what had happened more reasonably, find some closure, and then go back to living their separate lives.

Or maybe she would just barricade herself in his spare room and let him slip lettuce leaves under the door until the weather cleared and she could go home.

"All right," Rita finally conceded.

A *stalker?*

The word circled in Matthew's brain the whole time he and Rita fought the elements to make it home. And because the fierce weather meant they had no opportunity to talk, the word went deeper into his psyche with every new rotation. It continued to tumble through his thoughts as, side-by-side, they put together an impromptu dinner. The word distracted him even as they ate their meal together. In fact, his attention was diverted from the word only once, when the power went out and he had to go in search of candles.

Eating by candlelight did finally manage to budge Matthew's thoughts from the stalker business, but not in a way that was necessarily good—for either of them, because eating by candlelight roused all sorts of romantic implications that he was sure Rita was no more comfortable considering than he was. Nevertheless, he was helpless *not* to think in romantic terms after that. And not just because of the candlelit ambiance, either, but because Rita just looked so beautiful and so warm and so sexy, and she was here in his house again, effectively stranded for the whole night. When Matthew began to think about that, he could think of little other than what it would be like to make love to her again.

He would do it better this time, he promised himself. He would take more time with her, more care with her, and he would make sure her needs were met. Not that she had seemed dissatisfied last time—on the contrary, her climax had been as shudderingly complete as his own. But it could have been even better for her, he knew. And he certainly wouldn't end it this time by throwing her out of his house and sending her home alone. No, if they made love again, after it was over, he would pull her close and wrap her in his arms and murmur soft words and—

And never let her go.

It hit Matthew then, as he gazed at her across the candlelit table in his poshly decorated, but normally very empty-feeling dining room, that he really didn't want Rita ever to leave. They had spent the afternoon doing the mundane, everyday sort of things that couples do together—chatting, cooking, eating dinner—and even with the awkwardness that had arced between them, he'd enjoyed the experience more than he'd enjoyed anything for a very long time. Well, except for making love to Rita. But having spent the afternoon here in his home with her, he realized now just how solitary, how lonely, his life was without someone to share it.

And he realized, too, that the only person he would consider sharing it with was Rita Barone. Something about her just made him feel...better. Better about himself, better about his life, better about everything. Even though he'd botched things between them, he still felt better when he was with her. All he could do now, he thought, was to try to...un-botch things. He very much wanted to give whatever had been generated between the two of them two weeks ago—and maybe even before then—another chance.

But after dinner, with the power still out, when they were comfortably ensconced in front of a roaring fire sipping instant coffee spiked with good Irish whiskey—thank goodness the gas stove still worked so they could at least boil water—the word *stalker* rose up to taunt Matthew again. All this time, Rita had been thinking there was something sinister, perhaps even dangerous, behind those gifts for her.

What was she going to say and do when she found out the truth? How would she feel about Matthew then? Not that she necessarily harbored such great intentions toward him at the moment, he couldn't help thinking. But how was he supposed to tell her now that he had been the one who'd been leaving the gifts? Would she cast an even more distrustful eye on him? Worse yet, would she start thinking him sinister, perhaps even dangerous, too?

But then, could he blame her for thinking what she had? he asked himself. A beautiful single woman living alone in the big, bad city couldn't be too careful. He should have realized how she might misconstrue gifts from an anonymous admirer. Had he for a moment suspected she felt threatened by them, he would have identified himself a long time ago, and explained his actions.

Well, he would have done that if he *could* have explained his actions. He still wasn't entirely clear on all that.

Oh, the hell you're not, he chastised himself as he gazed

into the dancing, crackling flames and tried to think of something to say to Rita that would end the cumbersome silence lumbering between them. He was, too, clear on all that, he told himself further. Over the past two weeks, everything had become crystal-clear to him. He'd been leaving the gifts for her because he had a thing for Rita Barone—a major thing—and he'd been too scared to tell her. He'd been scared of being rebuffed by her if she ever found out. Scared of how humiliated he would feel when she rejected his attentions. She was Beauty, and he was the Beast. He'd been certain there was no way a woman like her would want anything to do with a man like him.

But she didn't rebuff you, he reminded himself. *She came home with you, and she made love with you. You. And no one else.*

He still wasn't sure why she had chosen him to be her first lover. He would have thought she would save that honor for someone special, someone who meant something to her. Someone with whom she intended to share her life. The way he'd often found himself wishing he could share his life with her.

His gaze shifted to the left then, to where they had placed their boots, side by side, on the hearth to dry. Near that were a couple of ladder-back chairs he'd pulled from the kitchen earlier for them to drape their coats over, likewise drying in the fire's heat. He'd changed his clothes when they'd arrived home, and was now dressed much as Rita was, in blue jeans and a heavy, whiskey-colored sweater. They sat on the floor in their stocking feet—side by side, but not too close—their backs propped against the leather sofa upon which they had made love two weeks before.

Neither had mentioned that, but Matthew was sure they'd both thought about it since entering the room and taking their current positions. That night had been full of passion and hunger and need. This evening, in the same place, with the same person, all he felt was comfort and coziness and camaraderie.

Interesting, not just that he and Rita could experience such divergent events and emotions in identical surroundings, but that he did indeed seem to be sharing his life with her right now. And she was sharing hers with him. And it felt very, very good.

"So tell me more about this stalker," he said, feeling more able to discuss that now than he had before, because he'd had time to deal with his surprise and didn't feel quite so flummoxed anymore.

And he did want to talk about it. He needed Rita to realize that there had been nothing threatening to any of the gifts. He wanted to assuage her fears. How to do that without revealing himself remained a mystery.

Then again, maybe he should reveal himself. Maybe he should tell her the truth about all of it. But how to do that and have it make sense remained a mystery, too. How could he make sense of it to her when he could scarcely make sense of it himself? And what would he do if, when Rita found out it was he who had left the gifts, she reacted badly? What if she misunderstood his intentions and thought him...odd...for doing it? What if she looked at him as if he were a creep, a freak—a beast?

He was going to have to tell her anyway, he decided. That was the only way she would realize there had been nothing sinister behind the gifts. Hopefully, an opportunity would arise during their conversation. Because if it didn't...

Well, he'd just have to figure out a way to make sure that it did.

He sensed, more than saw, her shrug in response to his request, because the only light in the room came from the warm, golden glow of the fire that barely reached out to surround them. Not to mention the fact that both of them seemed to prefer gazing into the fire instead of at each other.

"I've told you most of it," she said. "There's some guy at the hospital who's been leaving me gifts on special occasions, and I don't know who he is or why he's doing it."

"You're sure it's a guy?" Matthew asked, testing the waters.

"Well, I assume so," she said. "I can't see a woman doing that. Women are usually much more straightforward."

"Yeah, like Glenn Close in *Fatal Attraction*," he quipped.

"Please don't joke about it," Rita said, sounding distressed.

Matthew did turn to look at her then. And she responded by turning to meet his gaze. She really was scared of the person who had left the gifts, he realized.

How had everything gotten so messed up? he wondered. All he'd ever wanted was to do something nice for Rita Barone.

"I'm sorry," he apologized. Not just for making light of her fear, he thought, but for causing it in the first place. For too many things to name.

"It's just really got me rattled," she said, cupping both hands over her opposite arms, as if warding off a chill.

"Maybe it's just someone who wants to do something nice for you because you did something nice for him," Matthew suggested. That was a logical line of thinking, wasn't it? And it wouldn't necessarily incriminate him. Having noted the fear in both her voice and her body language, he was beginning to have second thoughts about identifying himself. He still wasn't sure where he stood with Rita, and he still dreaded being ridiculed and reviled if she found out the truth. If not by her, then by other people at the hospital. He wasn't sure he'd be able to handle it any better as an adult than he had as a child.

Rita shook her head. "I don't think so. I haven't done any good deeds lately," she said. "Nothing I wouldn't ordinarily do."

"Maybe what you consider an ordinary deed was an extraordinary deed to someone else," Matthew told her, recalling the way she had been with the homeless man, Joe. He'd certainly considered her efforts that day extraordinary. He never would have been able to soothe another human being the way Rita had that day. "Maybe this person just wants to show you that he thinks you're extraordinary yourself."

She smiled at that, a little sadly. "I'm not extraordinary in any sense of the word," she said resolutely.

And it was with no small degree of shock that Matthew realized she meant exactly what she said. She thought she was ordinary. Thought she was just like everyone else. She couldn't see what was the most obvious thing in the world.

"Of course, you are," he said before he could stop himself. But then he decided, What the hell, in for a penny, in for a pound. He turned his body to fully face hers. When she looked at him, he lifted a hand to cup it lightly over her jaw. "Rita," he said softly, gazing into her amazing brown eyes and holding on for dear life when he felt himself going under, "you're the most extraordinary woman I know. And if you can't see that, then it's no wonder you don't realize the truth about this so-called stalker."

Nine

Rita gazed back at Matthew in the faintly flickering, orange-golden light of the fire, totally confused by what he had just said. "What are you talking about?" she asked softly, her voice sounding shallow as it creased the mellow darkness.

He hesitated for only a moment, then told her, "I meant exactly what I said. That you're an extraordinary woman, Rita Barone."

She started to shake her head in denial, but that only served to turn her face more completely into his hand, intensifying the gentle caress of his fingertips against her skin. Heat thrummed through her midsection when she registered the soft touch, then spread slowly throughout the rest of her.

"Do you really think that?" she asked quietly.

This time he didn't hesitate before responding. "Yes. I do."

And then, before she even realized what he intended, Matthew dipped his head to hers and covered her mouth with his.

It was a kiss quite unlike any she had ever received, at once confident and tentative, demanding and exploratory. Somehow, she felt as if he were trying to tell her something as he kissed her, but that his feelings were a mix of emotions even he didn't quite understand.

Good, Rita thought as she kissed him back in the same way. That was good, because it put them on equal ground. She wasn't sure where this was going to lead, but somehow it felt right. It felt good. And she had gone too long feeling bad. For now, kissing Matthew was exactly what she wanted to do.

For long moments they only kissed, touching just where Matthew's fingers continued to stroke along the line of Rita's jaw. Again and again he dipped his head to hers, turning it first one way, then the other, as if he wanted to taste her from every angle. Eventually, she lifted a hand to his hair, threading her fingers gingerly through the silky chestnut tresses, loving the way they curled around her fingertips as if trying to trap her there. Then, little by little, he began to edge his body closer to hers, until she felt his thigh pressing into her thigh, and his hip nudging hers, and his shoulder brushing hers. With each move forward, he intensified the kiss, until it built into a fiercely burning embrace, one that threatened to blaze out of control.

No, Rita thought when she realized what was happening. Not again. She would not make love with a man who had thrown her out the last time they had come together this way. She tore her mouth from his and pushed her body away from him, then stood and moved to the fireplace, turning her back on him so that she was gazing at the fire and not his handsome, yearning face. One fire was hot enough, she told herself. There was no reason why they should start another one. Especially since it would go out all too soon.

She heard Matthew breathing raggedly behind her, but he made no move to follow her. "Rita?" he asked softly. "What's wrong?"

She realized then that her own breathing was as rough as his was, and she inhaled deeply in an effort to steady both it and her rapid heart rate. She heard sounds of movement behind her, but didn't know if he was standing up or only shifting positions. She swallowed hard, knowing she had to have an explanation for why he had asked her to leave after making love to her the night of the party. But she didn't know how to ask for it without sounding desperate and confused. Especially since desperate and confused was exactly how she felt at the moment.

"Matthew, can I ask you a question?" she finally said.

"Of course," he told her.

"The night of the party," she began. But she found it difficult to say anything more.

"Yes?" he spurred her.

Just ask him, she told herself. "After we..." She inhaled another breath and released it slowly. "After we...made love."

"Yes?"

"Why did you..." Ask him! "Why did you...make me leave?"

She heard more sounds of movement, seeming closer this time, then felt his presence immediately behind her. The fire threw wildly dancing shadows about the floor at her feet, and she could just make out part of Matthew's silhouette blending with her own. When she inhaled this time, she smelled him, too, the clean, masculine fragrance that was distinctly his.

His voice was as quiet as her mood when he replied. "I'm sorry about that," he said. "I shouldn't have done it."

"But why did you?" she insisted.

He hesitated another moment before telling her, "Because you didn't think I appreciated what happened between us. You didn't think I *could* appreciate it."

She turned around to face him, narrowing her eyes in confusion, shaking her head. "I never said that."

He looked sad and weary as he told her, "Yes, you did."

She searched her mind in an effort to recall whatever he thought he was talking about, then gasped softly when she finally remembered. She shook her head more firmly. "No. What I said was that I didn't think the fact that it was my first time would matter to you."

"Exactly," he said. "You didn't think I could appreciate the honor you were bestowing upon me."

"But—"

"When in fact, Rita," he continued, ignoring her objection, "there was nothing that could have mattered to me more."

"But—"

"And when you said you thought it wouldn't matter to me, it made me feel like you agreed with everyone at the hospital about me."

Now her eyebrows arrowed downward in bewilderment. "What do you mean?"

He lifted one shoulder and let it drop. "That you thought I was a beast, too. That I wasn't capable of having feelings for you."

"Oh, Matthew..."

"In fact I felt..."

He didn't finish whatever he had intended to say, only gazed at her as if she were the answer to every prayer he had ever sent skyward. She told herself to say something, do something, to show him how much he had come to mean to her. Then she made herself stop thinking and only allowed herself to feel. And her feelings in that moment were... Oh, so strong. She cupped her hand gently over his jaw, stroking her thumb over the skin grown warm from the fire and rough from a day's growth of beard. Then she lifted her other hand to the scars on his face that he thought made him so beastly, brushing her fingers gently over them, as well. Finally she pushed herself up on tiptoe and pressed her lips to his.

She kissed him in a way that she hoped he would understand meant she loved him. Because she was afraid to say the words out loud just yet. The feeling was still too new for her to understand it, still too fragile for her to share. But she wanted him to know how she felt. Kissing him the way she did was the only way she could think to do that right now.

He seemed to understand, though, at least some of it, because after a moment, he roped his arms around her waist and pulled her close and kissed her back with just as much feeling, just as much need, just as much promise. Rita's heart began to pound at the fierceness of the emotions racing through her. Never before had she felt like this. Not even that first night with Matthew. This was new, this was visceral, this was extraordinary.

Extraordinary, she thought again as she kissed him more deeply. That was what he had said she was. Extraordinary. That could only mean that he cared for her. But did he care for her as much as she cared for him? And did he want this feeling to last forever, as she did? Because Rita knew in that moment she never wanted to be apart from Matthew again.

Her thoughts drifted off into nothingness when he began

to tug at her sweater, and all she could do was eagerly lift her arms so that he could skim it up over her torso and shoulders and head. He tossed it carelessly to the ground when he did, then repeated the action for her thermal shirt. Then he unhooked her brassiere and slipped it down her arms and discarded it, as well. She wanted to cross her arms over her breasts, to hide herself, because she suddenly felt so vulnerable before him. But something in his eyes stopped her, something hot and hungry and needy. His gaze was fixed on her naked breasts, and she watched as, with aching slowness, he lifted one hand toward her again.

"You are so beautiful," he whispered roughly as he reached for her.

Gently, carefully, he traced the pad of his middle finger along the lower curve of her breast, then up the side, across the top, around again. With each new circle, he moved inward a little more, and with each new circle, Rita's heart pounded more rapidly. All she could do was stand there as he drew his invisible rings, and try, with little success, to keep her breathing under control. Eventually, he reached the center of her breast, hesitating only a moment before pushing the pad of his finger around her dark areola. Rita sighed with longing as he touched her, and he must have understood, because he closed his entire hand over her then, and dipped his head to hers for another eager kiss.

As he kissed her, Rita tugged at his sweater, too, jerking her mouth from his only long enough to yank the garment up over his lean abdomen and shoulders, then pull it completely over his head. As she discarded it to the floor, Matthew kissed her again, more passionately this time, tasting her deeply with his tongue. Blindly, she opened her hands over his naked shoulders, and then he was pulling her roughly against him, splaying his hands open over her bare back, rubbing his rough chest against her softer one.

The friction produced an almost unbearable heat, making Rita wonder if she might spontaneously combust. Instead of exploding, her fever only continued to intensify, and magnify, and multiply. Matthew, she could tell by the way he was touching her so needfully, hungrily, frantically, was experiencing the same sensations.

"I want you, Rita," he panted between kisses. "I want to make love to you again. I've missed you so much the past two weeks. Every night I dream about you. Dream about that one time we were together. I remember how you felt and tasted and smelled, and I remember what it was like to be buried deep inside you. And then I start wanting you again. Because I know that one time will never be enough. That I'll never have enough of you."

She told herself not to think about what he said, about what he meant. He wasn't telling her he wanted to be with her forever, she assured herself. He was only telling her he wanted to be with her again. She'd promised herself that the next time she made love to a man, it would be with one she intended to keep—and who intended to keep her— forever.

Then he kissed her again, long and hard and deep, and she could scarcely remember her own name, let alone any promises she had made to herself. When he kissed her like that, all she could remember was the way he had made her feel the night the two of them had come together in such a burst of urgency and conflagration. This time it was even more urgent, even more inflamed. She needed him even more now than she had before. Before, she hadn't known what she was missing, hadn't known how good it could be. Now, though, she did know that. She did remember, and she wanted to feel that way again. Oh, how she wanted it.

"I want you, too," she told him, not sure when she'd

decided to admit that, only knowing it was true. "Oh, Matthew, I want you so bad."

One corner of his mouth crooked up in something of a sly grin. "You want me bad, huh?" he echoed.

She could only nod in response to the fire she saw reflected in his eyes. Nod and feel as hot and wanton as he seemed to feel himself.

"Well, then, Rita," he murmured, "I'll do my best to be bad for you."

Oh, my, she thought.

And then he kissed her again, in a way that made it impossible for her to think at all. As he kissed her, he ran his hands over her back, cupping her shoulder blades, sketching her spine, tripping along her ribs one by one. Everywhere he touched her, he set off little fires of wanting. Rita explored him, too, loving the sensation of each rigid muscle her fingertips encountered on his broad back. His shoulders and arms were masses of solid sinew, too, and she marveled at how their bodies were so different, yet so complementary. Where he was hard, she was soft. Where he was rough, she was smooth. And where he was hot... Well, she was hot, too.

Now, she thought as she pulled her mouth reluctantly away from his. She wanted him now. Right now. Right here, in front of the fireplace, where the heat of the flames mirrored their own reaction to each other. But for some reason, she felt shy about undressing while he was watching her, so she turned her back as she reached for the button at her waistband of her jeans. Before she had the chance to unfasten it, though, Matthew stepped up behind her, pushing his body flush against hers, the coarse hair on his chest grazing her bare shoulder blades and sending a shiver of excitement rushing through her. The shiver turned to electricity, however, when he covered her hands with his and drew them away from her jeans.

"Let me do that," he whispered roughly near her ear as he moved his own hands to the place where hers had been.

Before she could answer, he dipped his head to the soft curve where her neck and shoulder joined, brushing his open mouth hotly over the tender skin there. Rita's eyes fluttered closed at the contact, and she was so wrapped up in enjoying the skim of his lips over her flesh that she barely noticed him slipping the metal button of her jeans through its denim hole. She reached one hand behind herself to tangle her fingers in his hair, and tilted her head to the side to facilitate the erotic exploration of his mouth. He uttered a soft, masculine sound, then slowly, oh so slowly, began pushing down the zipper of her jeans and spreading the fabric open wide.

Beneath, she wore brief cotton panties, but Matthew wasn't deterred for a moment. As he filled one hand with her breast again, he slipped the other beneath the supple cotton, pressing his palm against her flat belly, pointing his fingers downward, toward the heart of her femininity. Then, millimeter by leisurely millimeter, his fingers began a downward advance, halting momentarily at the edge of the downy curls between her legs. Rita gasped when she realized his intention, but Matthew was undeterred, moving his hand downward, pushing harder when the position of her blue jeans threatened to hinder his progress.

Instinctively, Rita took a small step to the side, widening her stance, giving him freer access to the prize he so clearly sought. When she did, he drove his fingers deeper, until he found his way to the damp folds of flesh and began to explore.

"Oh," Rita gasped when he touched her so intimately. "Oh, Matthew. That's so…"

"Do you like that?" he asked softly, his voice a damp caress against her ear.

"Oh, yes," she managed to pant. "Please... I want..."

"What?" he asked.

But all Rita could tell him was, "More..."

She wasn't sure, but she thought she heard him chuckle with much satisfaction as he drove his hand farther between her legs, fingering her gently, drawing erotic circles on her sensitive flesh and then tilling the tender folds with confident strokes. Her fingers tightened in his hair with each move he made, and she dropped her free hand to circle her fingers around his strong forearm, silently urging him to continue his erotic foray. So he did. Again and again he stroked his fingers over and along and between her, finally slipping one long digit inside her.

Rita gasped again at his scant penetration, then told him breathlessly, "I want you there. All of you, Matthew. I want you inside me again. Please, make love to me."

It was all the invitation he needed. After one final stroke, he removed his hand from her panties, dragging his damp fingertips up over her belly, and out to her hips. Then, without warning, he jerked her blue jeans and panties down over her hips, her thighs, her knees, baring her bottom and legs. Rita started to turn around to face him, but Matthew caught her hands in his and moved them to grip the mantelpiece instead. Reflexively, she clung to it, but looked over her shoulder to see him struggling with his own jeans. Quickly, but none too gracefully, he loosed the buttons of his fly and yanked down his pants. Then he stepped behind Rita and, gripping her hips in his hands, entered her from behind.

In spite of her position and the front-to-back love play in which they'd just indulged, she hadn't been expecting him to do that. Now to feel him push himself inside her the way he had, she was overcome with passion. Wanting. Heat. Need. He filled her so confidently, so adamantly, so completely, as if he and he alone had a right to be there. As if he belonged there. As if he were a part of her too long separated from her.

She knew then that he *was* a part of her. That he'd become a part of her that first night they'd made love. Because she had fallen in love with him that night. Totally, irrevocably in love. Maybe even before then, she thought vaguely as he withdrew himself and then pushed more deeply into her. Maybe that was why she had made love with him that night in the first place. Because on some deep, unconscious level, she had been in love with him all along.

He pulled out of her again, then entered her once more, and Rita pushed herself backward against him, until she felt as if he penetrated her to her very core. For some reason then, she vaguely recalled some misgiving she'd had after they'd made love the first time. Something about primary concerns and second thoughts. Something about precautions. Something about...

Pregnancy.

"Matthew," she managed to gasp. But she couldn't loose her hold on the mantelpiece, didn't want him to stop what he was doing, because it just felt so good. "We...we have to stop this. Now."

"What are you talking about?" he asked breathlessly against her neck. "We can't stop now."

She really didn't want to stop, either. Not when she was so close to... Not when they were so close to...

To maybe making a baby, she reminded herself brutally.

She made herself say what she had to say. "I could get pregnant," she told him softly.

He went still behind her, but didn't withdraw.

"We don't have any protection," she told him.

"We didn't have any last time, either," he said, his voice flat and even, belying nothing of what he might be thinking or feeling. And because she couldn't see him, she had no idea what his expression might tell her. "You could already be pregnant," he added with a surprising calmness in his tone.

She shook her head. "No. I've had my— Since then I've had evidence that I'm not. We were lucky."

"Were we?"

Weren't they? she wanted to ask him. But she was too muzzy-headed to figure it all out. "I don't want to take a chance again," she told him.

He hesitated, then she felt him nod. Carefully, he pulled out of her, then kissed her softly on her shoulder. "Upstairs," he said, "in the bathroom. I have some condoms. Meet me in my bedroom," he told her.

And then he was gone, melting into the darkness of the house as if he'd magically disappeared into the black beyond. Rita took a few deep breaths, telling herself she was too addle-brained from their loving to know what was going on. Nevertheless, she pushed her blue jeans and panties down around her ankles and stepped out of them, then pulled a ruby-red throw from the sofa and wrapped herself up in it. She had no idea where Matthew's bedroom was, but it was a safe bet that it was upstairs.

She made her way to the stairs, the fire offering her just enough light to find her way to the top. She looked left, then right. At the end of the hallway, a faint light glowed in one of the rooms, so she went toward it. The room was dark and masculinely furnished, a single candle burning on a mahogany antique dresser and the bedclothes on the massive sleigh bed turned back in invitation.

As she stepped in, Matthew slipped up behind her again,

wrapping his arms around her waist and burying his face at her nape to kiss her neck. "I thought you'd never get here," he murmured against her heated flesh.

She smiled as she reached behind herself to tangle her fingers in his hair. "It's only been a few minutes," she told him.

"It's been forever," he countered.

Slowly, he turned her around to face him, then urged the throw off her shoulders so that it pooled on the floor around her feet. Then he pulled her into his arms and kissed her deeply again, slowly walking her backward, toward the bed. She felt the mattress bump against the backs of her legs, then she was falling backward in the candlelit darkness, her feet still on the floor, with Matthew lying alongside her. Immediately, he rolled over onto his back, his feet still firmly planted on the floor, pulling Rita over with him until she lay atop him. After one final kiss, he cupped her shoulders with his hands and pushed her up, until she was kneeling over him, her legs on each side of his torso.

"You set the pace this time," he said. And then he covered her hips with his hands and smiled, a wicked, seductive little smile. He pushed her backward until her bottom made contact with his heavy, condom-encased shaft, then urged her up on her knees, positioning her over it. Inch by inch he brought her back down again, entering her slowly and deeply as he did. "You set the pace," he said again. "Fast or slow, deep or shallow, however you want it. Ride me, Rita."

Oh, merciful heavens, she thought. And then she realized she had no idea what to do.

She remembered that first time when he'd said he liked it fast and hard. But she wasn't sure she was ready for that. So, slowly, she pushed herself up on her knees again, then brought herself back down over him. Oh, that was so nice, she thought as she relished the slick friction of their bodies. Yes, slow and easy was definitely the way to go. For now.

Matthew didn't seem to mind, because he closed his eyes and lifted his hands to her breasts, filling his fingers with her. Rita opened her hands over his hard, muscular chest and lifted herself up again. She repeated the motion until both of them were breathing raggedly, their bodies glossy with sweat. Little by little, she increased the pace, gradually moving faster and harder over him.

Oh, yeah, she thought, there was definitely something to be said for doing it fast and hard, too.

Matthew moved his hands to her hips again, catching her rhythm, helping her pump against him more fiercely. Again and again he plunged into her, until she thought they would both explode from the heat their bodies were generating. A hot coil of pleasure began to tighten inside her, then, in a burst of fever, it began to consume her. As it did, he shifted their bodies again until Rita lay beneath him, and he hooked her legs around his waist. He took control of their coupling then, driving himself deep, deep inside her. Finally, with one last, fierce penetration, he cried out, going rigid and still above her. Rita, too, edged over the precipice then, her own climax culminating with his.

Then he collapsed alongside her, his breathing as labored and uneven as hers. For long moments they only lay there, their damp bodies entwined, their heat mingling, their thoughts scrambled. Then, weakly, Matthew began to push himself away. Instinctively, Rita reached for him, afraid he was about to do what he'd done before and tell her it was time for her to leave. He seemed to understand her fear, because he cupped his hand gently on her cheek and smiled, albeit a bit sadly.

"I'm not going to tell you to go," he said. "I just have to take care of our…precautions."

She closed her eyes, feeling stupid. Of course. But then, how was she supposed to know that? She wasn't exactly knowledgeable about this sort of thing. She lay quietly while Matthew was gone, marveling at what the two of them had just done, amazed that it could have been even better this time. And then he was with her again, lying beside her in the darkness, his body smooth and warm and hard, making her feel safe and pleasant and cherished. He lay on his side, one arm draped over Rita's waist, his hand gently cupping her breast. He stroked his thumb lightly over her nipple, and she shivered at the exquisite pleasure that shot through her in response.

"Cold?" he asked.

She shook her head. "Not at all," she told him.

"I can pull up the covers."

"No," she repeated. "I like being here with you like this." She turned on her side to look at him. "You have an amazing body, Dr. Grayson."

"In the dark," he qualified with a glance to the scant candlelight enveloping them. "In good light, it's not exactly a work of art."

She knew he was talking about his scars, and needing to prove to him that they didn't matter to her, she moved her hand to his shoulder, brushing her fingers over the puckered skin there with an affectionate caress.

"You're beautiful to me," she told him unequivocally.

He gazed at her silently for a moment, then reached for the hand she had opened over his scar. He withdrew it long enough to place a gentle kiss on her palm, then put it back where she had placed it before. But he offered nothing in response to her comment, only continued to gaze at her as if he couldn't quite believe she was real. Then he cupped his hand behind her head and pulled her toward him, kissing her again.

The kiss this time, though, was one of simple pleasure, a gesture meant to tell her how very happy he was that she was here with him.

"Stay the weekend with me," he said when he pulled away. "Stay until the storm is over."

Something twisted tight inside Rita at his words. Because although they were filled with longing and invitation, there was also an impermanence to them. He wanted her here until the storm passed, she told herself, but then what would happen?

"All right," she said, forcing a smile. "I will."

Inside, though, she was a mix of happiness and turmoil. She did indeed want to stay with Matthew until the storm was over. But that was because she knew the storm of her emotions was never going to end.

Ten

Rita stayed at Matthew's house until late Sunday evening, long after the great nor'easter ended, and long after the snowplows had cleared the streets. She wanted to stay even longer, but made herself return home for two reasons. One, so that she could sort through her feelings before going back to work. And two, because he hadn't invited her to stay any longer than the weekend.

Mostly, though, she did need to figure out what she felt for him. And she knew he needed time to himself, too, to try and make sense of his own emotions. Their weekend together had been an escape from reality in so many ways. On Monday morning, they would return to the real world of working with each other again, and she, at least, needed to be prepared, just in case Matthew decided to revert to his old beastly ways again.

She told herself that wasn't going to happen, especially after the way he kissed her good-night on the doorstep of her brownstone after driving her home, then placed the crystal bud vase holding her rose so carefully into her hand. Strangely, he hadn't asked her about the rose once over the weekend. But he had tended to it as carefully as she, making sure it had water and was placed in a sunny window. It had been just another enchanting aspect of their time together. There had been something magical about the snowstorm, something unearthly and illusory about the entire weekend. The real test, she knew, would come in the morning, when the two of them were thrust back into the workday world. She just hoped they both still felt the same way Monday morning.

But the first thing Rita saw on Monday morning was a note from Matthew that he had tucked into her mail slot. *I won't be in today,* the note read, *but meet me this evening for dinner, 7:00 at Darian's. We have to talk. Matthew.*

It was that last sentence that caused Rita the most concern. What did they have to talk about? she wondered. She folded the note and tucked it into the pocket of her scrubs with some trepidation.

Tonight, she supposed, she was going to find out.

The restaurant Matthew had chosen for dinner was one Rita had never visited before. Darian's was considered to be one of Boston's finer venues, but its prices were hard to manage on a nurse's salary. Yes, she was a member of the wealthy Barone family but she was unwilling to dip into her trust fund for something like dinner out.

Still, in light of the restaurant's reputation, she had dressed in her only outfit appropriate for such an establishment, the little black dress she'd worn to the party at Baronessa headquarters the night she and Matthew had made love for the first time. And if a not-so-little part of her was rather hoping this evening might have the same outcome as that one, well, that was just something she'd have to deal with. And she had. In fact, she'd dealt with it by wearing the same naughty lingerie she'd worn that night, too.

Well, a girl could dream, couldn't she?

Until the night of the blizzard, Rita had been so certain things with Matthew weren't going to work out, that the two of them had been finished before they could even get started. And after that night, she began to realize how very badly she did want them to work out. Before the party at Baronessa headquarters, she'd liked and admired him. Yes, he was gruff and standoffish, but she'd always sensed that there was a reason for that, something in his past that had wounded him and kept him from getting too close to anyone else. At the party, of course, she'd learned what that something was. And when she had realized the depth of the wounds from which he had had to recover—both physically and emotionally—she'd experienced a new kind of admiration for him. And she had begun to feel a sort of affection for him, too. Affection that had gradually grown into love.

There were many things the two of them had in common. They both took their work seriously, and were dedicated to their callings. He had a wry sense of humor, when he showed it, and he'd always seemed confident and reasonably content with his life. Rita had simply responded to him on a level she didn't with most people. She'd always felt comfortable around him, in spite of his seeming distance, and always felt better whenever he was around.

She remembered once, back before Christmas, when the nurses in CCU were passing a boring shift by taking turns answering the question "If you had to be stranded on a deserted island with someone from the hospital, who would you choose?" Most of the nurses had chosen a notoriously handsome intern, but when her turn had come, Rita had thought for a moment, then had said she thought Dr. Grayson would be a likely choice. The others hadn't bothered to hide their surprise that she would choose the beastly MD, and a few had outright called her nuts. But Rita had defended her choice, had told the other nurses she thought he would be good to have around because he was smart and self-sufficient and wouldn't panic.

What she hadn't told them that day was that she thought he was kind of attractive, sexy even, in his gruff, standoffish way.

Even back then, she realized now, she had been attracted to him. And the more she got to know him, the more appealing he'd become. Making love with him had finally made her understand how very much she *did* care for him. How much she had come to love him. The reason she had made him her first lover, she understood now, was because she had known on some subconscious level that he was indeed special. That he was someone she wanted to share her life with. That he was someone she wanted to share herself with. Because she had loved him. Even then.

All she could do at this point was hope that Matthew shared at least some of her feelings. She wasn't sure what she would do if he saw this as little more than a passing fling. She didn't think he did. He didn't seem the kind of man who would indulge in something so frivolous and superficial. But she wouldn't know for sure unless he offered her some kind of sign that what was happening between them meant as much to him as it did to her.

Of course, inviting a woman to the most expensive restaurant in town was certainly a good start, Rita thought as she pushed open the door to Darian's and entered. She saw Matthew immediately, waiting by the hostess stand, his gaze fixed on the door as if he hadn't wanted to take his eyes off it, lest he miss her entrance. He was wearing another one of his dark power suits with a white dress shirt and a conservative, berry-colored necktie, and although she had decided the other day that she preferred him in his more casual attire of jeans and sweater—or, better still, his even more casual attire of nothing at all—she went a little weak in the knees at the sight of him.

He was so incredibly handsome. And so charmingly unaware of the fact. And he was so gentle. And so sweet. How anyone could ever think him beastly was beyond her. She smiled a bit tentatively, feeling nervous for no good reason she could name.

"Hi," she said softly.

He smiled in response to her salutation, a slow, easy, very confident, very sexy smile. A small bubble of heat burst inside her, sending a warm sensation reeling throughout her entire system. After exhaling a small, soft sigh that felt very much like contentment, she strode forward and stopped beside him.

"You look beautiful," he said by way of a greeting.

She grinned. "You don't look so bad yourself," she replied.

Then he surprised her by leaning forward and covering her mouth with his. It was a brief, spontaneous show of affection, and she felt as if she would melt right there on the spot. It wasn't a lingering kiss, but it was a public kiss, a public avowal that she was important to him. Somehow, that pleased Rita down to the very depths of her soul.

He pulled back with obvious reluctance, but by then the hostess had returned and was telling them their table was ready, if they'd please just follow her. Matthew held Rita's chair for her as she took her seat, then, instead of moving to the other side of the table equipped for four, he sat down immediately to her right, as if he didn't want even the scant distance of a table separating them. That sensation of heat spread through Rita again. A server appeared immediately to take their drink orders, and after a quick glance at the wine list, Matthew ordered something red and full-bodied.

He seemed impatient about something, Rita thought as she watched him make the decision and place the order. Though not in any sort of negative way. She got the feeling there was something he wanted to discuss with her—but then, he'd said as much in his note—something she now realized must be very important. But he didn't seem to know how to go about approaching it.

"What?" she said, hoping to spur him. "What's wrong?"

He looked surprised by her question. "Wrong?" he echoed. "Nothing's wrong. Why would you ask that?"

She shrugged lightly, even though she didn't much feel light. "In your note, you said we needed to talk," she reminded him. "You must have something on your mind."

In response to her remark, Matthew only gazed at her in silence. And suddenly, Rita began to feel doubtful about what she had felt so certain of only moments ago. Could she have been wrong about the mood of the evening? she wondered. What if he really did see this as nothing more than a fling? What if, instead of an effort to cement their relationship, he intended tonight to be the big kiss-off?

"It's not that I have something on my mind," he finally said "It's that I have something in my pocket."

"What?" she asked warily.

He studied her in silence for a moment longer, then sat back in his chair and reached into the breast pocket of his jacket. Just as he was beginning to withdraw whatever was in there, however, their waiter returned with their wine and Matthew set his empty hand back on the table between himself and Rita. Their server went about placing their glasses meticulously on the table, taking such great care and time to do it just so, that Rita nearly jumped out of her chair to throttle him. Finally, however, he seemed to reach the proper level of feng shui because he smiled and nodded at both of them, offered a quiet, "I'll just give you a few more minutes to study the menu," then pivoted and walked away.

Rita turned her attention to Matthew, but he was diligently perusing his dinner choices. "The veal looks good," he said blandly.

Rita mentally gritted her teeth at him. Whatever he had been about to remove from his pocket, he was clearly planning to wait to show her now. So she, too, turned her attention to the menu, choosing the first item upon which her gaze fell.

"Rosemary-encrusted lamb chops," she muttered, looking back up at Matthew. "I'll have that. Now then, what was it you were saying?"

He glanced back up at her, seeming confused about something. Then his expression cleared. "Oh. The veal. I was saying it looks good."

Argh, Rita thought. "No, before that," she said. "We were talking about something else."

"Were we?"

"Yes, we were," she assured him, biting back her impatience. "You—"

But she never got to finish her thought, as their server returned again to take their orders.

She placed her order, then listened impatiently as Matthew wavered between the veal and the New York strip. Finally, he opted for, of all things, the beef medallions, something that sent their server scurrying off to do whatever it was servers did when they weren't annoying their patrons by interrupting their dialogues at the most inopportune moments. Rita took advantage of his absence to fold her elbows over the table and lean forward, blatantly invading Matthew's space.

"Before the veal," she said, striving for a patient tone, "you were about to say something else."

Matthew opened his mouth with the obvious intention of telling her that he couldn't remember, but Rita cut him off by lifting one hand, index finger extended.

"You said you had something in your pocket," she reminded him stoically. "Something you were about to take out and show me," she added, just in case he'd forgotten that part, too.

He made a soft tsk and nodded. "That's right," he concurred. "I remember now."

Finally, Rita thought.

"But maybe I should wait for dessert," he said.

She squeezed her eyes shut tight and silently counted to ten. "No," she said slowly and calmly when she opened them again, "you should tell me now."

When her gaze met his, she saw that his dreamy green eyes were fairly twinkling with mischief, and she realized he'd been deliberately stringing her along all this time.

She smiled knowingly. "C'mon," she said, turning her hand palm up now, and wiggling her fingers. "Let's have it," she said.

He continued to gaze at her for a moment longer, then leaned back in his chair again and reached into his jacket pocket once more. But he still hesitated a moment before withdrawing whatever was inside, and he suddenly seemed to be a little anxious about what he was doing. Slowly, though, he pulled his hand back out, cupping it over whatever he held so that Rita couldn't see it. Then he halted completely before showing her what it was.

"Close your eyes," he said.

She expelled a mildly exasperated sound. "Why?"

"Just do it," he told her.

She obeyed his edict, sitting back in her chair and folding her hands in her lap, then closing her eyes. She heard the soft shuffle of movement, then nothing.

"Okay," he said, his voice still laced with something akin to apprehension. "You can open them now."

When Rita did, she saw first Matthew's handsome face gazing back at her with what was clearly trepidation. Then, more curious than ever, she lowered her gaze to the table. There, sitting before her on the white china plate atop the white linen tablecloth was a small white box. A small white box tied up with gold ribbon.

Just exactly like the small white boxes tied with gold ribbon that her secret admirer/stalker had left for her in her mail slot at the hospital.

"What...?" And then she understood. It had been Matthew all along. He had been the one leaving her the anonymous gifts.

She jerked her head up to look at him, and understood then why he looked so worried. Because he was the one she had been concerned might be stalking her. Even after she had voiced that concern to him, even after she had told him how uneasy, even frightened, she was about the anonymous gifts, he hadn't told her the truth. And he was uncertain what her reaction would be, now that she did know the truth.

In all honesty, in that moment, Rita wasn't sure what her reaction was.

"It's been you all along?" she asked.

He nodded. "Yes." When she only continued to stare at him in silence, he blew out an impatient breath and tried to explain. "That first time," he began, "all I really wanted to do was to somehow say thank you for your help in the

E.R. that day with Joe, the homeless man. Do you remember that?''

Rita nodded. ''Yes,'' she said. ''But, Matthew, I was only doing my job that day. You didn't owe me any thanks.''

''I owed you more than you realize,'' he told her. ''You calmed the man down, and you made it possible for me to do *my* job. You also told him I was an excellent surgeon. The absolute best.'' He hesitated a moment before adding, ''And you told him I was a wonderful man. And when you said that, you sounded like you really meant it.''

''I did mean it,'' she told him.

He nodded. ''I know. That's why I felt like I needed to thank you. Because no one had ever said anything like that about me before. Certainly no one had ever meant it.''

''Oh, Matthew,'' she said, her heart turning over in spite of her dismay.

''When I left that first gift,'' he continued, ''I thought I left a note with it, explaining why it was there, telling you thanks for your help in the E.R. It wasn't until later, when I heard the rumors of your secret admirer, that I realized I had inadvertently forgotten to leave the note. It didn't even occur to me until later that it was Valentine's Day. And once everyone started talking about Rita Barone's secret admirer, I was too embarrassed to make myself known.''

''Because you weren't an admirer,'' she concluded.

He shook his head. ''No. Because I *was*.''

She eyed him curiously. ''But—''

''Looking back, I think maybe, subconsciously, I wasn't leaving you a gift to say thank you. I was leaving a gift to say I care about you. Because I did care about you then. I still do. That's why I left the other gifts, too.''

''On my birthday?'' she asked, even though she already knew the answer.

"Yes," he said.

"And the anniversary of my first day at the hospital?"

"Yes."

"And the rose, too," she said, making it a statement this time, not a question.

He nodded. "I wasn't sure you'd even make the connection with the date on that one, it having been two weeks since we made love. But you did," he added. "You were thinking about it that day, too."

"I've thought about it every day since it happened," she told him.

"Me, too."

She shook her head slowly, scarcely believing what he was telling her. "But how did you even know the anniversary of my first day working at Boston General?" she asked.

He inhaled deeply as he fixed his gaze on hers. "Because I remember that day very well," he said evenly. "I was in the E.R. when you reported for your first shift, and I remember how the first time you walked behind the nurses' station, the whole place just seemed to…light up, in reaction to your presence. And I remember every day that's passed since then, Rita. The day you came to Boston General was one of the most important days of my life."

She didn't know what to say, so she only asked, "Why?"

He leaned forward again, dropping his hands to the table, skimming one across the linen to cover one of hers. "Because that was the day that, for the first time since I was a child, I felt good inside."

She gaped softly at him. "What?"

He nodded. "It took me a while to figure it out, but there was just something about you that, from the first time I laid eyes on you, made me feel good again. And then, when

you didn't shy away from me that first time we were introduced, when you didn't even seem to notice my scars, I
knew you were someone special.''

"Why would that make me special? And why would I
shy away from you in the first place?" she asked. "I remember thinking how handsome you were the first time I
met you."

He eyed her dubiously. "Don't tell me you didn't notice
the scars."

"Of course I noticed them," she said. "But they didn't
matter to me."

He nodded. "And that's why you're so special," he said.
"Thinking back, I realize now that that was the moment I
began to fall in love with you."

For a moment, Rita was sure she had misheard what he'd
said. Or else, she had misunderstood. "But..." she began,
not daring to hope.

"Open the box," he said before she could finish, as if
he were afraid of hearing her answer.

"But—"

"Please, Rita," he said, a little more desperately. "Open
it. It will be the last one, I promise." His expression turned
a little grim. "One way or another. It will be the last."

She started to object again, but something in his expression halted her. She wanted to tell him she loved him, too,
but again, something made her stop. It seemed very important to him that she see what was in the little package
before she replied, so she turned her attention to it again.
It was a perfect cube, roughly two inches. Gingerly, she
picked it up, then carefully slipped off the gold ribbon. As
the white paper fell away, she saw a black velvet box beneath.

A jeweler's box, she couldn't help thinking.

She looked up at Matthew, and once again she opened

her mouth to say something. But he stopped her with a gesture, pointing at the box.

With trembling fingers, Rita did as he requested, folding back the top to see what was hidden beneath. Then she caught her breath at the ring inside. A perfect, heart-shaped diamond solitaire on a platinum band.

Holding the box in one shaky hand, Rita lifted her other to cover her mouth. And when she glanced up to look at Matthew, she felt two fat tears spill from her eyes to stream down her cheeks.

"Are you, um, proposing?" she asked weakly.

He smiled, expelling a single, hopeful chuckle. Instead of answering her question, though, he asked one of his own. "Are you accepting?"

"That depends," she told him.

His smile fell some. "On what?"

"On whether or not you actually said what I think you said a minute ago."

He looked confused. "About what?"

She sucked up all the nerve she had and said, "About falling in love with me."

Now he looked stunned. "Did I say something about that?" he asked.

She nodded, but her heart began to sink. "I thought you did. You said that when we first met and I didn't seem to notice your scars, that that was the moment you began to fall in love with me."

"Oh," he said, clearly bothered by the reminder. "I, um, I really shouldn't have said that."

Something went cold inside Rita at his response. And all she was able to manage in reply was a fragile-sounding, "Oh."

"I misspoke when I said that then," Matthew told her. "I'm sorry."

She nodded dispassionately, but inside, she was wondering if she could make it to the restaurant exit without falling apart. "I see," she said softly.

And just as softly, Matthew told her, "Because I meant to wait until now to say it."

A small flicker of heat sparked in Rita's midsection, and she snapped her gaze to meet his once again. "Say what?" she asked faintly.

He smiled. "That I love you. That I've loved you for years, even if I didn't realize it, and that I will continue to love you until I take my last breath. And that I want you to be there when that last breath leaves me." He held her gaze intently as he added, "So what do you say? Will you marry me, Rita Barone?"

She looked at him for a long time in silence, then, unable to help herself, she smiled back. "And here I've always thought you were so serious about everything."

He sobered some at that. "I am serious. About loving you, anyway. Rita, I—"

"Matthew, I—" she interjected at the same time.

He smiled again, though he still seemed uncertain. "You go first," he said.

She swiped a bent knuckle under first one eye, and then the other. "Oh, it was nothing," she told him. "I was just going to say I accept your proposal, that's all."

His smile then went supernova. "Oh, is that all?"

She nodded.

"And here I thought you were always so serious," he countered.

"I am," she readily assured him. "About wanting to marry you. You see, it seems I've fallen in love with you, too, somewhere along the way. Maybe I've loved you since that first moment, too. And I want to be with you for all the moments we have left."

It seemed all Matthew needed to hear, because without another word, he took the jeweler's box from her hand and plucked the ring from its velvet housing. Then he lifted her left hand to slip the ring down over her third finger.

"A perfect fit," he said as he completed the action.

"Yes, we are," she agreed.

He lifted her hand to his lips then, placing a chaste kiss first on the back, then in the center of her palm, a gesture that sent a shiver of heat shimmying through her. Then he lowered their hands back to the table, his palm up, and hers palm down against it. The ring caught the candlelight from the table and reflected it back in a dozen dazzling shades of orange and gold and blue, and Rita couldn't help thinking it was a sign of just how bright the future was for both of them.

"Oh, my brother Nicholas is going to be so happy," she said as she turned her hand first one way and then the other atop Matthew's, admiring the way the gemstone sparkled. "He always wanted me to marry a doctor."

Matthew chuckled. "Isn't it usually the mother who's pleased about that?"

"Oh, Mom will be thrilled, too," Rita promised him. "In fact, all the Barones will be thrilled." She looked up at Matthew then. "How about the Graysons?" she asked. "How are they going to feel about their venerable blue blood mixing with the new-American Barone blood?"

Matthew looked grave at that. "When I told my parents my intentions," he said in a very serious voice, "they were so upset about it, they broke a long-standing Grayson code."

"Uh-oh," Rita said. "That doesn't sound good."

Matthew nodded. "They broke down and they..." He inhaled a deep breath and released it slowly. "They smiled," he finished. "And then they did something really shocking."

Rita grinned. "What's that?"

Matthew shook his head in mock solemnity. "They hugged each other," he confessed. "And then they hugged *me*. It was quite a scene," he added. "But I'm the first to marry, see, and they've been wanting grandchildren for some time now."

Rita laughed. "Gee, I guess we'll just have to accommodate them there. Eventually," she added meaningfully. "I think I want you to myself for a while first."

"Sounds good to me, Ms. Barone."

"Soon to be Ms. Barone-Grayson," she said with a smile, entwining her fingers with his.

He nodded in approval. "That has a nice ring to it."

"Yes, it does," she agreed. And then she realized something that made her smile grow broader. "Oh, wow. It just now occurred to me, I'm the fourth Barone to get engaged this year. I think it's becoming a new family tradition. And you know, we Barones take family traditions very seriously. I wonder who'll be next?"

Matthew squeezed her hand gently in his. "I don't know," he said. "All I know is I love you and I can't wait to start our lives together."

"I love you, too," she vowed, dropping her gaze to their joined hands. "And I think, for dessert, we should go back to your place and have something very special."

"But they serve Baronessa Gelati here," he objected mildly. "Didn't you see it on the menu?"

She nodded. "But as much as I like Baronessa, there's something else I think we'd both rather have for dessert tonight."

He grinned. "What's that?"

She grinned back. "Each other."

"Well, gosh, why wait for dessert to have that?" he asked.

"Because I don't want to send our server into psychotherapy," she told him. "I don't think the poor guy could handle it if we just took off. He seems to take his job very seriously."

"If he has a good medical plan," Matthew said, "maybe his insurance will cover the cost of counseling."

Rita laughed. "Hey, I've got a good medical plan," she said. "One that involves a cardiologist and a nurse and some very naughty lingerie."

Before she could say another word, Matthew stood and reached back into his jacket, withdrawing his wallet this time. Then he tossed enough cash onto the table to cover their dinner and a tip. "Say no more," he told her.

"But don't you want to have dinner?" Rita asked as he moved behind her chair and pulled it—and her—out from the table.

"I'd rather have dessert first," he told her. "Lots and lots of dessert."

How could Rita possibly turn down an offer like that? She was, after all, a Barone. Dessert, she had always felt, was without question the best part of life. So, arm-in-arm, she and Matthew went home. To start the best part of their life together.

*   *   *   *   *

DYNASTIES: THE BARONES

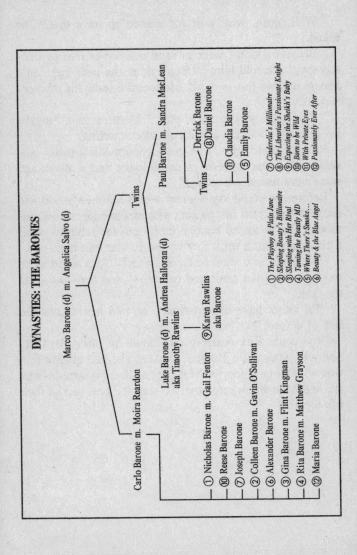

Marco Barone (d) m. Angelica Salvo (d)

Carlo Barone m. Moira Reardon

Luke Barone (d) m. Andrea Halloran (d)
aka Timothy Rawlins

Twins

Paul Barone m. Sandra MacLean

① Nicholas Barone m. Gail Fenton
⑩ Reese Barone
⑦ Joseph Barone
② Colleen Barone m. Gavin O'Sullivan
⑥ Alexander Barone
③ Gina Barone m. Flint Kingman
④ Rita Barone m. Matthew Grayson
⑫ Maria Barone

⑨Karen Rawlins
aka Barone

① *The Playboy & Plain Jane*
② *Sleeping Beauty's Billionaire*
③ *Sleeping with Her Rival*
④ *Taming the Beastly MD*
⑤ *Where There's Smoke...*
⑥ *Beauty & the Blue Angel*

Derrick Barone
⑧Daniel Barone

Twins

⑪ Claudia Barone
⑤ Emily Barone

⑦ *Cinderella's Millionaire*
⑧ *The Librarian's Passionate Knight*
⑨ *Expecting the Sheikh's Baby*
⑩ *Born to be Wild*
⑪ *With Private Eyes*
⑫ *Passionately Ever After*

DYNASTIES: THE BARONES
continues....
Turn the page for a bonus look
at what's in store for you
in the next Barones book—
only from Silhouette Desire!
#1507 WHERE THERE'S SMOKE...
by Barbara McCauley

One

Emily Barone stood in the small, back office of Baronessa Gelati and watched the single white piece of paper slowly roll into the copy machine tray, then lie flatly on top of the three other copies she'd already made. Light flickered on the dimly lit walls; the machine shuddered, then clicked to a stop.

It's not true, she told herself for the hundredth time. It can't be.

But Emily knew in her heart that the evidence she'd found against Derrick *was* true. There was no other explanation, nothing that could absolve, or forgive, what her brother had already done.

Or what he still planned to do.

Her hand shook as she reached for the incriminating piece of paper that proved Derrick's crime: he intended to sell secret recipes from the family gelato business to a rival company.

He'd been careful not to raise suspicion, Emily knew. Even as Derrick's secretary, Emily might not have ever noticed anything amiss if earlier today she hadn't accidentally overheard a few whispered words of a phone call on his private line, words that had made her uneasy. When he'd left his office a few minutes later, she'd gone in and pushed redial, only to hear a receptionist for Snowcream, Inc., Baronessa Gelati's biggest competitor, answer the phone.

She'd had to wait until the plant had closed this evening and everyone had left before she could search for evidence to confirm Derrick's betrayal. It had taken her nearly an hour to jimmy the lock on his desk, another fifteen minutes to find the file containing detailed notes from his conversation with Grant Summers, CEO of Snowcream. The files also contained dates and times Derrick had met with Summers, listed the amount of money to be exchanged for the information and the Swiss bank account the money would be transferred into.

Emily swallowed the lump in her throat and blinked back her tears. She knew she was naive. At twenty-four, she still tried to see the good in people, still hoped that in the end a person would do the right thing. She'd prayed she'd been wrong about Derrick, hadn't wanted to believe that her own brother would steal from anyone, let alone Baronessa Gelati.

At the sound of a door closing in an outer office, Emily froze. Quickly she reached across to the single table lamp she'd turned on when she came in. She stood in the dark, listening, heard a quiet, shuffling sound, then nothing. Slowly she moved toward the closed blinds over the small copy room window and peeked out through the side. She'd left the outer lights off, but she could see the outline of a tall, thin man at one of the desks.

She gasped as the man turned. Dear God! It was Derrick.

When he glanced in her direction, Emily jumped back. She'd never been a good liar. If he found her here, she knew she'd never be able to talk her way out. He'd only have to look at her face to know what she'd discovered, and he'd be furious. She couldn't confront him yet, not until she talked to Uncle Carlo.

Pressing her back to the wall, she waited until she finally heard the outer door close. Slowly she released the breath she'd been holding. To be sure he'd left the plant, she'd wait a while before she came out. She could take no chances that he might return and find her putting the file back in his desk, or discover her on her way out with the copies she'd made.

After several minutes, there were still no sounds, except for the soft ticking of the copy room wall clock and the beating of her own heart. The office was quiet. Thank goodness. She breathed a sigh of relief. She'd wait two more minutes and—

Once again she froze. And sniffed.

Smoke.

She flipped on the lamp again and glanced down. Thin ribbons of wispy gray smoke curled up from underneath the door.

Oh God, no—

She shoved the blinds apart and looked out. Flames shot up from the middle of the office and were spreading quickly across the room.

Why hadn't the alarm gone off? And why hadn't the sprinklers come on? Unless Derrick—

No! She couldn't believe that he would do such a terrible thing. Selling secret formulas was one thing, but arson was another. He couldn't—*wouldn't*—commit such a heinous crime.

She grabbed her purse and both files. There'd be no time to replace the original back into Derrick's desk, but she couldn't think about that now. She had to get out quickly, before the fire completely engulfed the office. Since there was no window to the outside from the copy room, she had no choice but to make a dash across the outer office and hopefully skirt the flames. If she could get to the windows overlooking the street two stories below, she could attract someone's attention. If worse came to worst—and she prayed it wouldn't—she would have to jump.

She gulped in air, then threw open the door and ran. A blast of heat made her stumble, but she recovered and kept going. In the distance she heard the wail of sirens and the sound gave her hope. They're coming, she thought as the wail and the deep sound of horns grew louder. They're almost here.

The fire crackled around her, sparks flew, singeing her face and bare legs. The smoke burned her throat and her eyes. But she made it to the window, and was reaching for the handle when the sound of a loud crack from behind her made her whip her head around. She watched in horror as the heavy steel bindings that supported the dropped ceiling gave way. Like a giant zipper opening, the ceiling ripped apart, raining metal and plaster tiles. Frantic, Emily turned back to the window, but the crack overhead rushed toward her like a hideous, furious monster.

Helpless to stop it, she went down.

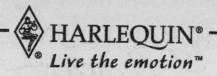
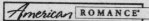

HARLEQUIN®
Presents

The world's bestselling romance series...
The series that brings you your favorite authors,
month after month:

Helen Bianchin...Emma Darcy
Lynne Graham...Penny Jordan
Miranda Lee...Sandra Marton
Anne Mather...Carole Mortimer
Susan Napier...Michelle Reid

and many more uniquely talented authors!

Wealthy, powerful, gorgeous men...
Women who have feelings just like your own...
The stories you love, set in exotic, glamorous locations...

HARLEQUIN®
Presents
Seduction and Passion Guaranteed!

HPDIR104

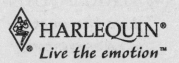

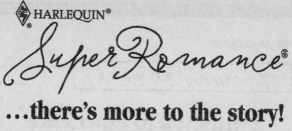
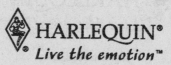

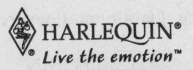

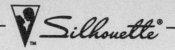

SPECIAL EDITION™

Emotional, compelling stories that capture the intensity of
living, loving and creating a family in today's world.

Desire

Modern, passionate reads that are powerful and provocative.

Romances that are sparked by danger and fueled by passion.

From today to forever, these love stories offer
today's woman fairytale romance.

BOMBSHELL™

Action-filled romances with strong, sexy, savvy women who save the day.